I psdulp Amgs

Bertha's Christmas Vision

Ao Avuvn o akgdh

I psdulp Arings

Bertha's Christmas Vision
An Autumn Sheaf

JaBS 1FAS / 8967779465468

Uslougf lo Fvspr g. b aA. Cdodf d. Avtusdrhd. Nr do

Cp, gs/ Hpup 4 Aof sgdt I Irbgek 1 r l: grhp©g

P psg d, dIrdbrg bppkt du **www.hansebooks.com**

"The little girl looked up gratefully, and thanked him for what she regarded as an act of kindness to herself."

P. 11.

BERTHA'S CHRISTMAS VISION

AN AUTUMN SHEAF

BY HORATIO ALGER JR.

Boston, Brown, Bazin, & co.

BERTHA'S

CHRISTMAS VISION:

An Autumn Sheaf.

BY HORATIO ALGER, JR.

BOSTON:
BROWN, BAZIN, AND COMPANY,
94, Washington Street.
1856.

BOSTON:
PRINTED BY JOHN WILSON AND SON,
22, School Street.

DEDICATION.

To my Mother.

As I turn over the pages of this my first book, and mark
here and there a name which use has made familiar, I feel the
more, that, but for your sympathy and encouragement,
much would still remain unwritten. With me you have
sorrowed over the untimely death of "Little Charlie."
"Bertha," with her precious gifts,—whereof so many stand
in need,—has grown to you and me not a child of fancy, but
a living presence. "Little Floy," and the "Child of the Street,"
will recall, to your mind as to mine, the touching lines of
Mrs. Browning:—

> "Do ye hear the children weeping, O my brothers!
>   Ere the sorrow comes with years?
> They are leaning their young heads against their mothers;
>   And *that* cannot stop their tears.
> The young lambs are bleating in the meadows;
>   The young birds are chirping in the nest;
> The young fawns are playing with the shadows;
>   The young flowers are blowing toward the West:
> But the young, young children, O my brothers!
>   They are weeping bitterly,—
> They are weeping in the play-time of the others,
>   In the country of the free.
> They look up with their pale and sunken faces,
>   And their looks are sad to see;
> For the man's grief abhorrent draws and presses
>   Down the cheeks of infancy."

To you, then, I dedicate this book,—which is partly
yours, in spirit, if not in deed,—confident, that, whatever
may be its shortcomings in the eyes of others, it will find a
kindly welcome at your hands.

CONTENTS.

LITTLE FLOY;
OR,
HOW A MISER WAS RECLAIMED.

Of all the houses which Martin Kendrick owned, he used the oldest and meanest for his own habitation. It was an old tumble-down building, on a narrow street, which had already lived out more than its appointed term of service, and was no longer fit to "cumber the ground." But the owner still clung to it, the more, perhaps, because, as it stood there in its desolation, unsightly and weather-beaten, it was no unfit emblem of himself.

Martin the miser! Years of voluntary privation, such as in most cases follow only in the train of the extremest penury, had given him a claim to the appellation. It might be somewhat inconsistent with his natural character, that, with the exception of the one room which he occupied, the remainder of the large house was left tenantless. After all, it was not so difficult to account for. He could not bear the idea of having immediate neighbors. Who knows but they might seize the opportunity afforded by his absence, and rob him of the gains of many years, which, distrusting banks and other places of deposit, he kept in a strong box under his own immediate charge?

Martin had not always been a miser. No one ever becomes so at once; though doubtless the propensity to it is stronger in some than in others. Years ago,—so many that at this time the recollection only came to him dimly, like the faint sound of an almost-forgotten tune,—years ago, when the blood of youth poured its impetuous current through his veins, he married a fair girl, whose life he had shortened by his dissipated habits; and the indifference, and even cruelty,

9

to which they led.

The day of his wife's death, the last remnant of the property which he inherited from his father escaped from his grasp. These two events, either of which brought its own sorrow, completely sobered him. The abject condition to which he had reduced himself was brought vividly to his mind; and he formed a sudden resolution, —rushing, as will sometimes happen, from one extreme to the other, —that, as prodigal as his past life had been, that which succeeded should be sparing and penurious in the same degree; until, at least, he had recovered his losses, and, so far as fortune went, was restored to the same position which he had occupied at the commencement of his career.

But it is not for man to say, "Thus far shalt thou go, and no farther," —to give himself up, body and soul, to one engrossing pursuit, and, at the end of a limited time, wean himself from it.

Habit grows by what it feeds on. It was not long before the passion of acquisition acquired a controlling influence over the mind of Martin Kendrick. He reached the point which he had prescribed for himself; but it stayed him not. Every day his privations, self-imposed though they were, became more pinching, his craving for gold more insatiable. Long ago, he had cut himself off from all friendship, —all the pleasures and amenities of social intercourse. He made no visits, save to his tenants, and those only on quarter-day. Nor were these of an agreeable character to those favored with them; for Martin was not a merciful landlord. He invariably demanded the uttermost farthing that was due; and neither sickness nor lack of employment had the power for a moment to soften his heart, or delay the execution of his purpose. His mind was drawn into itself, and, like an uncultivated field, was left to all the barrenness of desolation. Such is always the case, when a man, by his own act, shuts himself out from his kind, foregoes their sympathy and kind offices, and virtually says, "I am sufficient unto myself."

Martin had one child, a girl, named Florence. At the time of the death of her mother, she was but six years old. He had loved her, perhaps, as much as it was in his power to love any one; and, as long as she remained with him, he did not withdraw himself so entirely from human companionship. But, at the age of seventeen years, she became acquainted with a young man, a mechanic, in whose favor her affections were enlisted. He proposed for her hand; but her father, in whom love of gold was strong, on account of his poverty drove him, with scorn, from his door.

The young man was not to be baffled thus. He contrived to meet Florence secretly, and, after a while, persuaded her to forsake her home, and unite her fortunes with his,—with the less difficulty, since that home offered but few attractions to one of her age. Her father's indignation was extreme. All advances towards reconciliation, on the part of the newly-wedded pair, were received with a bitterness of scorn, which effectually prevented their repetition. From that time, Martin Kendrick settled down into the cold, apathetic, and solitary existence which has been described above. Gradually the love of gain blotted out from his memory the remembrance of his children, whom he never met. They had removed from the city, though he knew it not; and the total amount of interest displayed respecting them discouraged any idea they might have entertained of informing him.

"It's a cold night," quoth Martin to himself, as he sat before the least glimmering which could decently be called a fire in the apartment which he occupied. He cast a wistful glance towards a pile of wood which lay beside the grate. He lifted one, and poised it for a moment, glancing meanwhile at the fire, as if he was debating in his mind whether he had best place it on. He shook his head, however, as if it were too great a piece of extravagance to be thought of, and softly laid it back. He then moved his chair nearer to the fire as if satisfied that this would produce the additional warmth without the drawback of expense.

It was, indeed, a cold night. The chill blasts swept with relentless rigor through the streets, sending travellers home with quickened pace, and causing the guardians of the public peace, as they stood at their appointed stations, to wrap their overcoats more closely about them. On many a hearth the fire blazed brightly, in composed defiance of the insidious visitor who shuns the abodes of opulence, but forces his unwelcome entry into the habitations of the poor.

A child, thinly clad, was roaming through the streets. Every gust, as it swept along, chilled her through and through; and at length, unable to go farther, she sank down at the portal of Martin Kendrick's dwelling. Extreme cold gave her courage; and, with trembling hand, she lifted the huge knocker. It fell from her nerveless grasp, and the unwonted sound penetrated into the room where Martin sat cowering over his feeble fire. He was startled, terrified even, as that sound came to his ears, echoing through the empty rooms in the old house.

"Who can it be?—robbers?" thought he, as he walked to the door. "I will wait and see if it be repeated."

It was repeated.

"Who's there?" he exclaimed, in a somewhat tremulous voice, as he stood with his hand upon the latch.

"It's me," said a low, shivering voice from without.

"And who's 'me'?"

"Floy, —little Floy," was the answer.

"And what do you want here at this time of night?"

"I am freezing. Let me come in and sit by the fire, if only for a moment. I shall die upon your steps."

The old man deliberated.

"You're sure you're not trying to get in after my money, what little I have? There isn't any one with you, is there?"

"No one. There is only me. Oh, sir, do let me in! I am so cold!"

The bolt was cautiously withdrawn; and Martin, opening a crack, peered forth suspiciously. But the only object that met his gaze was a little girl, of ten years of age, crouching on the steps in a way to avail herself of all the natural warmth she had.

"Will you let me come in?" said she, imploringly.

"You had better go somewhere else. I haven't much of a fire. I don't keep much, it burns out fuel so fast. You had better go where they keep better fires."

"Oh, sir, the least fire will relieve me so much! and I haven't strength to go any farther."

"Well, you may come in, if you're sure you haven't come to steal any thing."

"I never steal: it's wicked."

"Umph! Well, I hope you'll remember it. This is the way."

He led her into a little room which he occupied. She sprang to the fire, little inviting as it was, and eagerly spread out both hands before it. She seemed actually to drink in the heat, scanty as it was, so welcome did it prove to her chilled and benumbed limbs.

A touch of humanity came to the miser, or perhaps his own experience of the cold stimulated him to the act; for, after a few minutes' deliberation, he took two sticks from the pile of fuel, and threw them upon the fire. They crackled and burnt; diffusing, for a time, a cheerful warmth about the apartment. The little girl looked up gratefully, and thanked him for what she regarded as an act of kindness to herself.

"Fuel's high, very high; and it takes a fearful quantity to keep the fire agoing."

"But what a pleasant fire it makes!" said the little girl, as she looked at the flames curling aloft.

"Why, yes," said Martin, in a soliloquising tone, "it is comfortable; but it would not do to have it burn so bright. It would ruin me completely."

"Then you are poor?" said the little girl, looking about the room. The furniture was scanty; consisting only of the most indispensable articles, and those of the cheapest kind. They had all been picked up, at second-hand stores, for little or nothing.

It was no wonder that little Floy asked the question. Nevertheless, the miser looked suspiciously at her, as if there was some covert meaning in her words. But she looked so openly and frankly at him as quite to disarm any suspicions he might entertain.

"Poor?" he at length answered. "Yes, I am; or should be, if I plunged into extravagant living and expenses of every kind." And he looked half regretfully at the sticks which had burned out, and were now smouldering in the grate.

"Well," said Floy, "I am poor too, and so were father and mother. But I think I am poorer than you; for I have no home at all, no house to live in, and no fire to keep me warm."

"Then where do you live?" asked the miser.

"I don't live anywhere," said the child, simply.

"But where do you stay?"

"Where I can. I generally walk about the streets in the daytime; and, when I feel cold, I go into some store to warm myself. They don't always let me stay long. They call me ragged, and a beggar. I suppose," she continued, casting a glance at her thin dress, which in some places was torn and dirty from long wearing, — "I suppose it's all true; but I can't help it."

"Where do you think of going to-night?" asked Martin, abruptly.

"I don't know. I haven't any place to go to; and it's very cold. Won't you let me stay here?" asked the child, imploringly.

The miser started.

"How can you stay here? Here is only one room, and this I occupy."

"Let me lie down on the floor, anywhere. It will be better than to go out into the cold streets."

The miser paused. Even he, callous as his heart had become, would not willingly thrust out a young girl into the street, where in all probability, unless succor came, she would perish from the severity of the weather.

After a little consideration, he took the fragment of a candle which was burning on the table, and, bidding Floy follow him, led the way into a room near by, which was quite destitute of furniture, save a small cot-bed in the corner. It had been left there when Martin Kendrick first took possession of the house, and had remained undisturbed ever since. A quilt, which, though tattered, was

15

still thick and warm, was spread over it.

"There," said Martin, pointing it out to Floy, who followed him closely, — "there is a bed. It hasn't been slept on for a great many years; but I suppose it will do as well as any other. You can sleep there, if you want to."

"Then I shall have a bed to sleep in!" said Floy, joyfully. "It is some time since I slept on any thing softer than a board, or perhaps a rug."

Martin was about to leave her alone, when he chanced to think the room would be dark.

"You can undress in the dark, can't you?" he inquired. "I haven't got but one light. I can't afford to keep more."

"Oh! I sha'n't take off my clothes at all," said the young girl. "I never do."

She got into bed, spread the quilt over her, and was asleep in less than five minutes.

Martin Kendrick went back to his room. He did not immediately retire to bed, but sat for a few minutes, pondering on the extraordinary chance—for in his case it was certainly extraordinary—which had thrown a young girl, as it were, under his protection, though but for a limited time. He was somewhat bewildered, so unexpectedly had the event happened, and could scarcely, even now, realize that it was so.

But the warning sound of a neighboring church-clock, as it proclaimed midnight, interrupted the train of his reflections, and he prepared for bed; not neglecting, so strongly was the feeling of suspicion implanted in him, to secure the door by means of a bolt. When he awoke, the sun was shining through the window of his room. He had hardly dressed himself, when a faint knock was heard at the door of his room. Opening it a little ways, he saw Floy

16

standing before him.

"What! you here now?" he inquired.

"Yes. Where should I go? Besides, I did not want to unlock the front door without your permission."

"That is quite right," said Martin. "Some one, who was ill-disposed, might have entered and stolen,—that is, if he could have found any thing worth taking."

"And now, sir, if you please, I'll make your bed," said the child, entering the room. "I've made the one I slept in."

Martin looked on without a word; while Floy, taking his silence for assent, proceeded to roll back the clothes, shake the bed vigorously, and then spread them over again. Espying a broom at one corner of the room, she took it, and swept up the hearth neatly. She then glanced towards the miser, who had been watching her motions, as if to ascertain whether they met with his approval.

"So you can work?" said he, after a pause.

"Oh, yes! mother used to teach me. I wish," said she, after a while, brightening up, as if struck with a new idea,—"I wish you would let me stay here: I would make your bed, take care of your room, and keep every thing nice. Besides, I could get your dinners."

"Stay with me! Impossible. I don't have much to do: besides, I couldn't afford it."

"It won't cost you any thing," said Floy, earnestly. "I know how to sew; and, when I am not doing something for you, I can sew for money, and give it to you."

This idea seemed to produce some impression upon the old miser's mind.

"But how do I know," said he, a portion of his old suspicions returning,—"how do I know but you will steal off some day, and carry something with you?"

"I never steal," said Floy, half indignantly. "Besides, I have no place to go to, if I should leave here."

This was true; and Martin, considering that it would be against her interest to injure him in any such way,—an argument which weighed more heavily than any protestations on her part would have done,—at length said, —

"Well, you may stay,—at least, a while. I suppose you are hungry. There's a loaf of bread in the closet. You may eat some of it; but don't eat too much. It's—it's hurtful to the health to eat too much."

"When will you be home to get some dinner?" asked the child.

"About noon. Perhaps I will bring some sewing for you to do."

"Oh, I hope you will! It will seem so nice not to be obliged to be walking about the streets, but to be seated in a pleasant room, sewing!"

When Martin came home at noon, instead of finding the room cheerless and cold, as had been his wont, the fire was burning brightly, diffusing a pleasant warmth about the apartment. Floy had set the table in the centre of the room, —with some difficulty it must be confessed; for it was rickety, and would not stand even, owing to one of the legs being shorter than the rest. This, however, she had remedied by placing a chip under the deficient member. There was no cloth on; for this was an article which Martin did not number among his possessions. Floy had substituted two towels, which, united, covered perhaps half the table.

A portion of the loaf—for there was but one—she had

toasted by the fire, and this had been placed on a separate plate from the other. On the whole, therefore, though it was far from being a sumptuous repast, every thing looked clean and neat; and this alone adds increased zest to the appetite. At least, Martin felt more of an appetite than usual; and, between them, the two despatched all that had been provided.

"Is there any more bread in the closet?" asked Martin.

"No," said Floy: "it is all gone."

"Then I must bring some home when I return to supper."

"I have been thinking," said Floy, hesitatingly, "that, if you would trust me to do it, and would bring home the materials, I would make some bread; and that would be cheaper than buying it; and, besides, it would give me something to do."

"What!" asked Martin, as he looked, with an air of surprise, at the diminutive form of little Floy, "do you know how to make bread? How came a child like you to learn?"

"Mother used to be sick a good deal," said Floy, "and was confined to her bed, so that she could do nothing herself. She used to direct me what to do; so that, after a while, I came to know how to cook as well as she."

"Well, what shall I have to bring home?" asked the miser, whom the hint of its being cheaper had enlisted in favor of the plan.

"Let me see," said Floy, as she sat down and began to reflect: "there's flour and saleratus and salt. But we've got the salt; so you need only get the first two."

"Very well; I will attend to it. Oh! I forgot to ask what sewing you knew how to do. Can you make shirts?"

"Yes; I have made a good many."

19

"Then I will bring you home some to-night, if I can get any."

When she had cleared away the dinner-dishes, washed them, and put them in the closet,—an operation which the simplicity of the meal rendered but a short one,—Floy began to look round her, to see what else she could do. A desire seized her to explore the old house, of which so many rooms had for years remained deserted. They were bare and desolate, inhabited only by spiders and crickets, who occupied them rent free. It might have been years, perhaps, since they had echoed to the steps of a human foot. They looked dark and gloomy enough to have been witness to many a dark deed of midnight assassination. But it was all fancy, doubtless; and in little Floy they produced no other feeling than that of chilliness. She rummaged all the closets with a feeling of curiosity, but found nothing in any one of them to reward her search until she came to the last. There was a large roll of something on the floor, which, on examination, proved to be a small carpet, quite dirty, and somewhat moth-eaten. It had probably been left there inadvertently, and remained undiscovered until the present moment. Floy spread it out, and examined it critically. An idea struck her, which she hastened to put into execution. Threading her way back to the miser's room, she procured a stout stick which stood in the corner, and, going back, gave the carpet a sound drubbing, which nearly stifled her with dust. Nevertheless, she persevered, and soon got it into quite a respectable state of cleanness. She then managed, by a considerable effort, to lug it to Martin's room, and, in an hour or so, had spread it out, and finally fastened it by means of some tacks which she found in one corner of the closet. The effect was certainly wonderful. The carpet actually gave the room a very cosy and comfortable appearance; and little Floy took considerable credit to herself for the metamorphosis.

"What will he say?" thought she. "I wonder whether he will be pleased."

It was but a few minutes after this change had been effected that Martin came in. It was about three o'clock,— sooner than Floy expected him; but he had thought she might require the materials early, in order to make preparations for the evening meal.

As he opened the door, he started back in surprise at the changed appearance of the room. It occurred to him, for a moment, that he had strayed into the wrong place; but the sight of Floy, sitting at the window, re-assured him, and he went in.

"What is all this?" he inquired in a bewildered tone.

Floy enjoyed his surprise. She told him in what manner she had effected the change, and asked him if he did not like it.

He could not do otherwise than answer in the affirmative; and, in truth, an unusual sense of comfort came over him as he sat down and looked about him.

Floy had taken possession of the flour, and was already kneading it.

"Now," said she, after this was done, "I must put it down by the fire to rise; that will not take long; and then it will be ready to bake."

"Have you got any shirts for me?" she inquired after a while.

"Yes," said Martin, recollecting himself, and unrolling a bundle which he had placed on the table. "There are half a dozen for you to begin on; and, if you do them well, you can have some more."

Floy looked pleased.

"Now," said she, "I shall have something to do when you are away."

"You like to be doing something?" said Martin, inquiringly.

"Oh, yes! I can't bear to be idle."

Martin did not go out again that afternoon. About six o'clock, Floy set the table, and placed upon it a plate of warm cakes which might have pleased the palate of an epicure. It was the best meal the miser had tasted for years, and he could not help confessing it to himself. Floy was gratified at the appetite with which he ate.

Thus matters went on. The presence of the little girl seemed to restore Martin to a part of his former self. He was no longer so grasping and miserly as before. Through little Floy's ministry, he began to have more of a relish for the comforts of life, and less to grudge the expense necessary to obtain them.

It was not many weeks before he fell sick, in consequence of imprudent exposure to the rain. At first he did not regard it; but a fever set in, and he was confined to his bed.

At the urgent solicitation of Floy, he consented to have a physician called, though not without something of reluctance at the thought of the fee.

Then it was that he began to appreciate more fully the importance of Floy's services. Ever ready to minister to his wants, no one could wish a more faithful or attentive nurse. As she sat by his bedside in the long days through which his sickness was protracted, busily engaged with her sewing, he would lie for hours, watching the motion of her busy fingers with pleased interest. Occasionally—for he had nothing else to do—his mind would wander back to the scenes of his early manhood, and he would sigh over the recollection of the happiness which might have been his. Then his thoughts would be borne along the dreamy years which had intervened, unlighted by the rays of friendship, and uncheered by the presence of affection. The image of his daughter, whom he had cast off, and of whose after-fate he knew nothing, came up before him, and he could not repel it. A change, a beneficial and salutary change, was rolling over his mind, —the fruit of those long involuntary hours of sickness and self-communing.

On the first day succeeding his recovery, he invited Floy to go out with him. It was an unusual request, and Floy hardly knew what to make of it. She got her bonnet, however (for shawl she had none), and complied. It was a chilly March day, and the thin dress which she had worn from the time of her coming to Kendrick's was but an ill protection against the weather. She shivered involuntarily.

"You are cold," said Martin; "but you will not need to go far."

He led the way into a dry-goods store.

"Have you any warm shawls suitable for a little girl?" he inquired. He selected one, and paid for it. "Show me some dress-patterns," he continued.

Two different ones were chosen. Martin paid for them.

"Can you direct me," he inquired, "to any good dressmaker's?"

The clerk had at first been inclined to laugh at the old man, whose attire, though warmer, was no better looking than Floy's; but the promptness with which he paid for his purchases, and the glimpse which had in this way been obtained of a well-filled pocket-book, inspired him with a feeling of respect, and he readily complied with his request.

"Now," said Martin cheerfully to Floy, "we will have you

a little better dressed, so that you need not fear the cold."

"I am sure," said Floy, gratefully, "that I am much obliged, and I don't know how I can repay you."

"You have already," said the old man with feeling. "I don't know how I should have got along without you when I was sick."

"Floy," said Martin, thoughtfully, as they came out from the dressmaker's, "although you have been with me for some time, I have never thought to ask your name,—I mean your other name besides Floy."

"My name is not Floy," said the child. "They only call me so. My real name is Florence,—Florence Eastman."

"Florence Eastman!" said the old man, starting back in uncontrollable agitation. "Who was your mother? Tell me quick!"

"Her name," said the child, somewhat surprised, "was Florence Kendrick."

"Who was her father?"

"Martin Kendrick."

"And where is he? Did you ever see him?"

"No," said Floy, shaking her head. "He was angry with mother for marrying as she did, and would never see any of us."

"And your mother?" said Martin, striving to be calm. "Is she dead?"

"Yes," said Floy, sorrowfully. "First, my father died, and we were left very poor. Then mother was obliged to work very hard, sewing; and finally she took a fever, and died, leaving me alone in the world. For a week, I wandered about without a home; but at last you took me in. I don't know what would have become of me if you had not," said she, gratefully.

"Floy," said Martin, looking at her steadfastly, "do you know my name?"

"No," said Floy. "I have often wondered what it was, but never liked to ask you."

"Then," said he, in an agitated tone, "you shall know now. I am Martin Kendrick, your GRANDFATHER!"

Floy was filled with amazement, but, after a moment, threw herself into his arms. "Will you forgive mother?" she asked.

"I will! I have! But, alas! she has much more to forgive me. Would that she were still alive!"

Every day, Martin Kendrick became more alive to the claims of affection. His miserly habits gave way, and he became more considerate in his dealings with his tenants. The old house, in which he lived so many years, was torn down; and he bought a neat cottage just out of the city, where he and Floy live happily together. Floy, who has been sent to school, exhibits uncommon talent, and is fitting for the station she will soon assume as the heiress of her grandfather.

MY CASTLE.

"I have a beautiful castle,
  With towers and battlements fair;
And many a banner, with gay device,
  Floats in the outer air.

"The walls are of solid silver;
  The towers are of massive gold;
And the lights that stream from the windows
  A royal scene unfold.

"Ah! could you but enter my castle,
  With its pomp of regal sheen,
You would say that it far surpasses
  The Palace of Aladeen;—

"Could you but enter as I do,
  And pace through the vaulted hall,
And mark the stately columns,
  And the pictures on the wall;—

"With the costly gems about them,
  That send their light afar,
With a chaste and softened splendor,
  Like the light of a distant star!"

"And where is this wonderful castle,
  With its rich emblazonings,
Whose pomp so far surpasses
  The homes of the greatest kings?"

"Come out with me at morning,
  And lie in the meadow-grass,
And lift your eyes to the ether blue,
  And you will see it pass.

"There! can you not see the battlements;
  And the turrets stately and high,
Whose lofty summits are tipped with clouds,
  And lost in the arching sky?"

"Dear friend, you are only dreaming;
　Your castle so stately and fair
Is only a fanciful structure, —
　A castle in the air."

"Perchance you are right. I know not
　If a phantom it may be;
But yet, in my inmost heart, I feel
　That it lives, and lives for me; —

"For, when clouds and darkness are round me,
　And my heart is heavy with care,
I steal me away from the noisy crowd,
　To dwell in my castle fair.

"There are servants to do my bidding;
　There are servants to heed my call;
And I, with a master's air of pride,
　May pace through the vaulted hall.

"And I envy not the monarchs
　With cities under their sway;
For am I not, in my own right,
　A monarch as proud as they?

"What matter, then, if to others
　My castle a phantom may be,
Since I feel, in the depth of my own heart,
　That it is not so to me?"

MISS HENDERSON'S
THANKSGIVING DAY.

Thanksgiving Day dawned clearly and frostily upon the little village of Castleton Hollow. The stage which connected daily with the nearest railroad station (for as yet Castleton Hollow had not arrived at the dignity of one of its own) came fully freighted, both inside and out. There were children and children's children, who, in the pursuit of fortune, had strayed away from the homes where they first saw the light; but who were now returning, to revive, around the old familiar hearth, the associations and recollections of their early days.

Great were the preparations among the housewives of Castleton Hollow. That must indeed be a poor household which, on this occasion, could not boast its turkey and plum-pudding,—those well-established dishes; not to mention its long rows of pies,—apple, mince, and pumpkin, —wherewith the Thanksgiving board is wont to be garnished.

But it is not of the households generally that I propose to speak. Let the reader accompany me, in imagination, to a rather prim-looking brick mansion, situated on the principal street, but at some distance back, being separated from it by a front yard. Between this yard and the fence ran a prim-looking hedge, of very formal cut, being cropped in the most careful manner, lest one twig should, by chance, have the presumption to grow higher than its kindred. It was a two-story house, containing in each story one room on either side of the front door; making, of course, four in all.

If we go in, we shall find the outward primness well

supported by the appearance of things within. In the front parlor—we may peep through the door, but it would be high treason, in the present moistened state of our boots, to step within its sacred precincts—there are six high-backed chairs standing in state, two at each window. One can easily see, from the general arrangement of the furniture, that from romping children, unceremonious kittens, and unhallowed intruders generally, this room is most sacredly guarded.

Without speaking particularly of the other rooms,— which, though not furnished in so stately a manner, bear a family resemblance to "the best room,"—we will usher the reader into the opposite room, where he will find the owner and occupant of this prim-looking residence.

Courteous reader! Miss Hetty Henderson. Miss Hetty Henderson, let me make you acquainted with this lady (or gentleman), who is desirous of knowing you better.

Miss Hetty Henderson, with whom the reader has just passed through the ceremony of introduction, is a maiden of some thirty-five summers, attired in a sober-looking dress of irreproachable neatness, but most formal cut. She is the only occupant of the house, of which, likewise, she is proprietor. Her father, who was the village physician, died some ten years since; leaving to Hetty,—or perhaps I should give her full name, Henrietta,—his only child, the house in which he lived, and some four thousand dollars in bank-stock, on the income of which she lived very comfortably.

Somehow, Miss Hetty had never married; though, such is the mercenary nature of man, the rumor of her inheritance brought to her feet several suitors. But Miss Hetty had resolved never to marry,—at least, this was her invariable answer to matrimonial offers; and so, after a time, it came to be understood that she was fixed for life,—an old maid.

What reasons impelled her to this course were not known; but possibly the reader will be furnished with a clew before he finishes this narrative.

Meanwhile, the invariable effect of a single and solitary life combined attended Hetty. She grew precise, prim, and methodical, to a painful degree. It would have been quite a relief if one could have detected a stray thread even upon her well-swept carpet; but such was never the case.

On this particular day,—this Thanksgiving Day of which we are speaking,—Miss Hetty had completed her culinary preparations; that is, she had stuffed her turkey and put it in the oven, and kneaded her pudding; for, though she knew that but one would be present at the dinner, her conscience would scarcely have acquitted her if she had not made all the preparations to which she had been accustomed on such occasions.

This done, she sat down to her knitting; casting a glance every now and then at the oven, to make sure that all was going on well. It was a quiet morning; and Miss Hetty's thoughts kept time to the clicking of her knitting-needles.

"After all," thought she, "it's rather solitary taking dinner alone, and that on Thanksgiving Day. I remember, a long time ago, when my father and my brothers and sisters were living, what a merry time we used to have round the table. But they are all dead; and I—I alone—am left."

Miss Hetty sighed; but, after a while, the recollections of those old times returned. She tried to shake them off; but they had a fascination about them, after all, and would not go at her bidding.

"There used to be another there," thought she,—"Nick Anderson. He too, I fear, is dead."

Hetty heaved a thoughtful sigh, and a faint color came

into her cheeks. She had reason. This Nicholas Anderson had been a medical student, apprenticed to her father; or rather placed with him, to be prepared for his profession. He was perhaps a year older than Hetty, and had regarded her with more than ordinary warmth of affection. He had, in fact, proposed to her, and had been conditionally accepted on a year's probation. The trouble was, he was a little disposed to be wild, and, being naturally of a lively and careless temperament, did not exercise sufficient discrimination in the choice of his associates. Hetty had loved him as warmly as one of her nature could love. She was not one who would be drawn away beyond the dictates of reason and judgment by the force of affection. Still, it was not without a feeling of deep sorrow,—deeper than her calm manner led him to suspect,—that, at the end of the year's probation, she informed Anderson that the result of his trial was not favorable to his suit, and that henceforth he must give up all thoughts of her.

To his vehement asseverations, promises, and protestations, she returned the same steady and inflexible answer; and, at the close of the interview, he left her, quite as full of indignation against her as of grief for his rejection.

That night, his clothing was packed up, and lowered from the window; and, when the next morning dawned, it was found that he had left the house, never, as was intimated in a slight note pencilled and left on the table in his room, to return again.

———————————

While Miss Henderson's mind was far back in the past, she had not observed the approach of a man, shabbily attired, accompanied by a little girl apparently some eight years of age. The man's face bore the impress of many cares

31

and hardships. The little girl was of delicate appearance; and an occasional shiver showed that her garments were too thin to protect her sufficiently from the inclemency of the weather.

"This is the place, Henrietta," said the traveller at length, pausing at the head of the gravelled walk which led up to the front door of the prim-looking brick house.

Together they entered; and a moment afterwards, just as Miss Hetty was preparing to lay the cloth for dinner, a knock sounded through the house.

"Goodness!" said Miss Hetty, fluttered. "Who can it be that wants to see me at this hour?"

Smoothing down her apron, and giving a look at the glass to make sure that her hair was in order, she hastened to the door.

"Will it be asking too much, madam, to request a seat by your fire for myself and little girl for a few moments? It is very cold."

Miss Hetty could feel that it *was* cold. Somehow, too, the appealing expression of the little girl's face touched her. So she threw the door wide open, and bade them enter.

Miss Hetty went on preparing the table for dinner. A most delightful odor issued from the oven; one door of which was open, lest the turkey should overdo. Miss Hetty could not help observing the wistful glance cast by the little girl towards the tempting dish as she placed it on the table.

"Poor little creature!" thought she. "I suppose it is a long time since she has had a good dinner."

Then the thought struck her, "Here I am alone to eat all this. There is quite enough for half a dozen. How much these poor people would relish it!"

By this time the table was arranged.

"Sir," said she, turning to the traveller, "you look as if you were hungry as well as cold. If you and your little daughter would like to sit up, I should be happy to have you."

"Thank you, madam!" was the grateful reply. "We are hungry, and shall be much indebted to your kindness."

It was rather a novel situation for Miss Hetty,—sitting at the head of the table, dispensing food to others beside herself. There was something rather agreeable about it.

"Will you have some of the dressing, little girl? I have to call you that; for I don't know your name," she added, in an inquiring tone.

"Her name is Henrietta; but I generally call her Hetty," said the traveller.

"What!" said Miss Hetty, dropping the spoon in surprise.

"She was named after a very dear friend of mine," said he, sighing.

"May I ask," said Miss Hetty, with excusable curiosity, "the name of this friend? I begin to feel quite an interest in your little girl," she added, half apologetically.

"Her name is Henrietta Henderson," said the stranger.

"Why, that is my name!" ejaculated Miss Hetty.

"And she was named after you," said the stranger, composedly.

"Why, who in the world are you?" she asked, her heart beginning to beat unwontedly fast.

"Then you don't remember me?" said he, rising, and looking steadily at Miss Hetty. "Yet you knew me well in bygone days,—none better. At one time, it was thought you

33

would join your destiny to mine——"

"Nick Anderson!" said Miss Hetty, rising in confusion.

"You are right. You rejected me because you did not feel secure of my principles. The next day, in despair at your refusal, I left the house, and, ere forty-eight hours had passed, was on my way to India. I had not formed the design of going to India in particular; but, in my then state of mind, I cared not whither I went. One resolution I formed,—that I would prove by my conduct that your apprehensions were ill founded. I got into a profitable business. In time, I married; not that I had forgotten you, but that I was solitary, and needed companionship. I had ceased to hope for yours. By and by, a daughter was born. True to my old love, I named her Hetty, and pleased myself with the thought that she bore some resemblance to you. Afterwards my wife died; misfortunes came upon me; and I found myself deprived of all my property. Then came yearnings for my native soil. I have returned (as you see), not as I departed, but poor and care-worn."

While Nicholas was speaking, Miss Hetty's mind was filled with conflicting emotions. At length, extending her hand frankly, she said,—

"I feel that I was too hasty, Nicholas. I should have tried you longer. But, at least, I may repair my injustice. I have enough for us all. You shall come and live with me."

"I can only accept your generous offer on one condition," said Nicholas.

"And what is that?"

"That you will be my wife!"

A vivid blush came over Miss Hetty's countenance. She "couldn't think of such a thing," she said. Nevertheless, an hour afterwards the two united lovers had fixed upon the marriage-day.

———————————

The house does not look so prim as it used to do. The yard is redolent with many fragrant flowers. The front door is half open, revealing a little girl playing with a kitten.

"Hetty," says a matronly lady, "you have got the ball of yarn all over the floor. What would your father say if he should see it?"

"Never mind, mother; it was only kitty that did it."

Marriage has filled up a void in the heart of Miss Hetty. Though not so prim, or perhaps careful, as she used to be, she is a good deal happier. Three hearts are filled with thankfulness at every return of MISS HENDERSON'S THANKSGIVING DAY.

———————————

LITTLE CHARLIE.

A violet grew by the river-side,
    And gladdened all hearts with its bloom;
While over the fields, on the scented air,
    It breathed a rich perfume.
But the clouds grew dark in the angry sky,
    And its portals were opened wide;
And the heavy rain beat down the flower
    That grew by the river-side.

Not far away, in a pleasant home,
    There lived a little boy,
Whose cheerful face and childish grace
    Filled every heart with joy.
He wandered one day to the river's verge,
    With no one near to save;
And the heart that we loved with a boundless love
    Was stilled in the restless wave.

The sky grew dark to our tearful eyes,
    And we bade farewell to joy;
For our hearts were bound by a sorrowful tie
    To the grave of the little boy.
The birds still sing in the leafy tree
    That shadows the open door:
We heed them not; for we think of the voice
    That we shall hear no more.

We think of him at eventide,
    And gaze on his vacant chair
With a longing heart, that will scarce believe
    That Charlie is not there.
We seem to hear his ringing laugh,
    And his bounding step at the door;
But, alas! there comes the sorrowful thought, —
    We shall never hear them more!

We shall walk sometimes to his little grave,
    In the pleasant summer hours;
We will speak his name in a softened voice,
    And cover his grave with flowers;
We will think of him in his heavenly home, —
    His heavenly home so fair;

And we will trust with a hopeful trust
That we shall meet him there.

BERTHA'S CHRISTMAS VISION.

It was the night before Christmas. Snow was falling without; and the wind dashed the cold flakes, in eddying whirls, into the faces of those wayfarers whom business or pleasure kept out thus late. They drew their warm garments more closely about them, and hurried onward; little heeding the pelting of the storm while the vision of a cheerful hearth and a merry family circle danced before their eyes and warmed their hearts. Merry St. Nicholas, too, the patron saint of children, was abroad. It was a busy night with him. Thousands of parcels must be made up, and showered down as many chimneys into expectant stockings, before the morrow's dawn. So he gives the reins to his coursers, and speeds swiftly along, —

"through forest and brake;
Through deep, drifting snow; over river and lake;
Over hill, over dale, where the keen northern blast,
With fierce, angry moaning, drives fearfully past."

In a large and pleasant room sat little Bertha, gazing thoughtfully into the fire. The fire crackled and burnt; and shadows, cast by its flickering light, danced on the wall. But little Bertha's thoughts were far away, and she heeded them not. For many weeks, she had been looking forward to this very night; and now she was trying to conjecture what gifts good St. Nicholas had in store for her. At length she grew weary of conjecture, took a lamp from the table, and went up stairs to bed. It was a neat little chamber; and the counterpane on Bertha's bed rivalled in whiteness the falling snow without. Bertha looked out of the window, against the panes of which the snow was beating noisily.

"It is a cold night," thought she. "St. Nicholas will have a

39

hard time of it. What if he should not come at all?"

Bertha's apprehensions were soon dispelled; for, as she looked out, the sound of silvery bells came nearer and nearer, till at length it paused under her window, and, a moment afterwards, was heard in an opposite direction. Bertha rubbed her eyes, and strove to distinguish the sleigh from which these sounds proceeded; but she could distinguish nothing.

"Can it be St. Nicholas?" thought she.

Even as she spoke, mingling with the sound of the retreating bells, she thought she could distinguish the words of a song. She listened attentively; and these were the words which the wind bore to her: —

"The path I have chosen
    Is covered with snow;
The streams are all frozen;
    Yet onward I go.

"I glide o'er the mountain,
    And skim o'er the lea;
I pass by the fountain;
    Yet no eye can see —

"My form or my shadow
    On snow-drift or mound,
On hill-top or meadow,
    Or frost-spangled ground.

"While sleigh-bells are ringing
    Upon the highway,
And glad parties singing
    So thoughtless and gay, —

"I pass through and over
    Each hamlet and hall
Ere mortals discover
    Who gave them a call.

"I pause but to count o'er

> The gifts for each one,
> And then quickly mount o'er
> The stile. I am gone!"

"That must certainly be Santa Claus," thought Bertha. So she carefully hung up her stockings before the fire, and went to bed. She soon became tired of waiting for St. Nicholas to come; and, in a few minutes, she was asleep. But the thoughts of Christmas had taken fast hold of her mind, and, as she slept, shaped themselves into the following dream: —

She thought, that, as she was lying awake in her chamber, there appeared suddenly before her three figures, clad in white. Slowly they advanced, hand in hand, till they stood before her bedside. Then, with united voices, they chanted the following lines: —

> "Maiden, from the fields of air
> We have winged our rapid flight,
> Bringing gifts both rich and rare,
> On this frosty Christmas night.
> Guard them ever: they will be
> Of exceeding worth to thee."

They ceased; and Bertha, in great astonishment, inquired, —

"What! are you St. Nicholas? Or," she added, recollecting herself, "perhaps you are his sisters?"

The visitors resumed their chant: —

> "Maiden, no! Thy Christmas saint
> Beareth gifts of mortal taint:
> At the touch of sure decay
> They shall vanish quite away.
> Those we bear are not of earth:
> Theirs has been a higher birth."

The visitors ceased; and one of their number, coming

41

forward, commenced anew: —

"I am Faith. To thee I bear
  Childlike trust and confidence
In the ever-watchful care
  Of our Father's providence.
Maiden, one of sisters three,
This the gift I bear to thee."

The second came forward, and repeated: —

"I am Hope. When darksome clouds
  Gather round thy earthly way,
And Misfortune's shadowy veil
  Intercepts the light of day,
I will come on wings of light:
  Clouds and mist shall straightway fly,
And reveal the golden gates
  Of a happier home on high.
Maiden, one of sisters three,
This the gift I bear to thee."

Smiling graciously on the wondering Bertha, Hope drew back, and gave place to her sister, who commenced as follows: —

"I am Charity. Let me
  Ever on thy steps attend,
And, as long as life shall last,
  Be thy counsellor and friend.
In thy bosom I would sow
  Seeds of gentleness and love,
And, a resident of earth,
  Fit thee for a home above.
Maiden, last of sisters three,
This the gift I bear to thee."

Again the sisters joined hands, and, with united voices, chanted, as at first, —

"Maiden, from the fields of air
  We have winged our rapid flight,
Bringing gifts both rich and rare,

On this frosty Christmas night.
Faith and Hope and Charity!
Earthly maiden, sisters three,
These the gifts we bear to thee."

Their voices died away, and they were gone. Bertha opened her eyes, and, lo! it was all a vision that had come to her on this Christmas night. The morning sun was shining brightly through the window-panes. Noisily over the frozen snow dashed the sleighs; and their bells rang a merry peal in honor of Christmas Day. Bertha glanced at the well-filled stockings that hung in front of the fire, and then she knew that St. Nicholas had been there with his budget of gifts; and the words sung by the sisters came into her mind: —

"Maiden, no! Thy Christmas saint
Beareth gifts of mortal taint.
Those we bear are not of earth:
Theirs has been a higher birth."

"I will not forget the gifts of the good sisters," she murmured softly. "Doubtless it is my heavenly Father who has sent them to me."

So it was that little Bertha, attended by the three sisters, walked peacefully and happily through life.

The ways of God's providence, so dark and mysterious to many, became plain and clear to her; for she saw with the eye of Faith. Clouds sometimes gathered about her path; but Hope waved her wand, and they were at once dispelled. Jealousy and envy and angry thoughts disturbed her not; for her heart was filled with the heavenly spirit of Charity.

Would that we all might be blessed with Bertha's Christmas vision!

WIDE-AWAKE.

Many years ago, in a city whose name I cannot now recall, there lived a poor woman, whose husband had died, leaving nothing but a little son. For some time, she continued to support herself, and her son, whom she dearly loved, by working early and late at the spinning-wheel. But, after a while, a heavy misfortune fell upon her: it was no less than the loss of eyesight. So she was obliged to give up her spinning; for now she could distinguish neither the web nor the woof. You can imagine her distress at being deprived so suddenly of seeing the great and beautiful spectacle of fields, flowers, and sky, which every day presents to our gaze. Still, she would not have heeded all this; but she found herself cut off, at the same time, from all means of subsistence.

Meanwhile, her son had grown up into a stout, active boy of twelve. He was full of life and animation; and that, I suppose, was the reason he had received the name of "Wide-awake." Now, little Wide-awake had a kind heart as well as manly spirit; and when he saw that his mother, who had worked so hard and so long for him, had become blind, he said to himself, "Now it is my turn to work."

So he told his mother that he was going to seek for work, and that, after three months, he would faithfully return. But first he sold the spinning-wheel, which was no longer of any use, and one or two other articles, and gave the money to a neighbor, who promised to spend it for his mother as she had need. Then he took a cheerful leave of his mother, and went off with a light heart, though his pockets were empty.

He had not walked far when he overtook an old woman,

who was bending beneath the weight of a heavy burden. She was homely, and appeared very tired. Wide-awake was passing by, when she called out to him, "Come here, little boy: help me to carry this bundle. I am old, weak, and tired; you are young and strong."

Wide-awake was very obliging; and, though the old woman's tone was not the pleasantest in the world, he very willingly took one side of the bundle, and helped her to carry it. The day was hot, and the bundle heavy; but he bore up stoutly, so that the old woman began to get over her ill humor, and to ask him some questions. So he told her his whole story,—how his mother was blind and unable to work, and he was seeking his fortune.

"Well," said the old woman, "if that is the case, I think you had better come and live with me. I live in a little cottage not far off, and am in want of a boy to go on errands and do other little things for me. If you will come and stay with me three months, I will reward you as you deserve. But I will warn you that I am very particular, and shall require you to obey me in every thing."

Of course, Wide-awake was only too glad to accept the old woman's offer. He was quite sure that he should be able to suit her; and he could not help picturing to himself how glad his mother would be to have him return with perhaps a piece of gold; for this seemed a great sum to Wide-awake, and a very generous compensation for three months' labor.

After a while, they came to the old woman's cottage. It was a small house, containing three rooms. One of these was a kitchen, in which the old woman did all her cooking; another was her chamber; and the third she told Wide-awake he should have to sleep in.

Early the next morning, the old woman came to his bedside, and shook him roughly.

"Up! up!" said she. "Is not the sun up? and you are lying here asleep! What is your name?"

"Wide-awake," said he, rubbing his eyes.

"Then," said the old woman, "hereafter, be sure to be wide awake before the sun. Dress yourself as quickly as possible, and I will give you your breakfast; and then to work."

Wide-awake was up and dressed in a moment. The old woman set before him a bowl of bread and milk for his breakfast. After he had eaten this, she took him to a fold near by, where he saw ten beautiful sheep.

"These," said she, "will be your care. You will drive them to the great meadow a mile hence, and watch them, taking care that none stray away. Three times a day—at morning, noon, and night—you will drive them to the spring, and let them drink; and, at seven o'clock, you may bring them back."

Wide-awake promised faithfully to obey her in every respect. He found the great meadow without difficulty. He watched the sheep, and watered them, as he had been directed, and, at nightfall, drove them home. The old woman counted the sheep, and, finding them all there, was well content, and gave Wide-awake his supper.

So time passed on. Every day the old woman became better satisfied with Wide-awake, who, on his part, was looking forward to the time when he might go home.

One morning about this time, as Wide-awake was about to drive out his sheep as usual, the old woman stopped him.

"They have grown quite fat," said she; "so I shall carry them to the city and sell them. I shall be gone a week, and shall leave you here to take care of the house while I am gone. You will not have much to do. But there is one thing I must warn you against: you must not, on any account, open the door of the closet which is in your chamber. If you do, you will repent it."

Wide-awake was not troubled with curiosity; and so he found no difficulty in making this promise.

The old woman departed, and Wide-awake was left alone. Having nothing else to do, he began to think of home and his mother. Then he began to wonder how much his mistress meant to give him for his services. He determined that he would buy a nice arm-chair for his mother, and a great many other things, if his money only held out. But they were all for his mother's comfort, and not for his own, as I have already explained that Wide-awake was far from being selfish.

On the fourth day after the old woman's departure, a stout man came to the door, and asked leave to rest a little while. Wide-awake knew that his mistress would have no objection; so he gave him permission, and, moreover, placed before him some bread and milk. The man ate heartily, and, in the mean time, contrived to draw out of Wide-awake all the particulars of his situation, and the old woman's prohibiting him to open the door of the closet.

"I have no doubt," said he, "that it is there where she keeps her money. If I were in your place, I would look and see. It wouldn't do any harm."

"But," said Wide-awake, in astonishment, "she told me not to do it on any account."

"Never mind that," said the man, winking: "it'll do no harm; and she'll never know it."

"But," said Wide-awake, firmly, "I have promised; and I never break my promise."

"Well, then, if you won't, I will," said the stranger, rising;

"for I'm determined to know what there is in that closet."

But Wide-awake sprang to the door, set his back resolutely against it, and said,—

"Never! while I live."

"Poh!" was the contemptuous reply. "What is your strength against mine? Don't you know that I can kill you?"

"That may be," said Wide-awake, firmly,—though the thoughts of his mother came over his mind; and he could not help sighing for her, if he should die,—"but I will not yield."

"Are you quite determined you will not let me in?" said the stranger.

The voice seemed altered; and, looking up, Wide-awake beheld, to his great surprise, that it was the old woman who addressed him.

"Where is the man who was here a minute since?" asked he in surprise.

The old woman smiled, and explained to him that she was a fairy, and had taken a man's figure to test his sincerity. She said she was quite satisfied with the result, and, as she had no further need of his services, would let him return home.

"But I owe you something for your past fidelity. What shall it be? I leave it to your choice. Wealth, happiness, and long life: I will confer either of these upon you. Choose."

"And may I choose any thing I like?" said Wide-awake, with eyes sparkling.

"Yes," said the fairy (for so we must now call her).

"Then I will choose that my mother be restored to sight."

"You have chosen well, my child," said the fairy, kindly:

"it shall be as you say; and, to reward you for your affection to your mother, I will freely bestow upon you the three gifts which you did not choose. You shall be rich; and your life shall be both long and happy."

Wide-awake found his mother fully restored to sight. With the wealth which the fairy bestowed upon him, he built a neat cottage for his mother, who was long spared to him. The fairy's promise was verified in every particular.

THE FIRST TREE
PLANTED BY AN ORNAMENTAL TREE SOCIETY.

We have planted it deep in the yielding soil,
    Hard by the house of prayer;
And the cool air plays through its leafy top,
    As it stands in silence there.

It is young like ourselves; but, day by day,
    The dews of heaven will fall, —
And the gladsome rays of the summer sun,
    That shines for each and all;
And, under their gentle ministry,
    It will grow both stout and tall.

Then will the roots of the stately tree
    Have spread both far and wide;
And perchance its branches will overtop
    The church that stands beside;
And safe amid its clustering leaves
    Will summer birds abide.

And those who, full of youthful life,
    About the sapling played,
With sober mien and whitened locks
    Will stand beneath its shade,
And ponder with a thoughtful brow
    On the changes Time has made.

The years will roll, with a steady course,
    To meet Time's infinite sea;
And the silent waves, in their fearful sweep,
    Will ingulf both you and me;
But still, like a beacon that tells of the past,
    Will stand our first elm-tree.

THE ROYAL CARPENTER OF
AMSTERDAM.

The superintendent of the Dock Yard in Amsterdam was seated in his office one afternoon, indulging himself in smoking a rude pipe; a luxury then recently imported from the colony of Virginia, in the New World.

His reflections, whatever they were, were broken in upon by a knock at the door,—not a timid, hesitating knock; but a bold, authoritative summons. The superintendent, judging it must proceed from some person of consequence, hastily laid aside his pipe, and quickly threw open the door, to admit his unknown visitor.

Instead of the high personage he anticipated, he beheld standing before him a stout man, of commanding person, and dressed in the attire of a workman.

He was a little vexed to think he had been so much deceived; and perhaps it was natural that he should accost the intruder in a somewhat peevish manner.

"Well, my good man, what do you want, that you come thumping at the door as if you were really a man of mark? What would you have?"

"I seek employment," said the stranger in a deep voice, not at all intimidated at his reception.

At the same time, he presented a letter to the superintendent.

"Ha!" said the latter, glancing at it with considerable surprise; "from the Russian ambassador!"

He read aloud as follows:—

53

"Sir,—The bearer, a countryman of mine, is desirous of obtaining employment in the Dock Yard under your superintendence. He is not altogether unacquainted with this description of labor, but wishes to perfect himself in it. I feel assured that nowhere can he do so to greater advantage than under your instruction."

The compliment implied in the concluding sentence served to moderate the vexation occasioned by his recent misapprehension; and he turned with a milder mien to his visitor.

He was a little surprised to find, that, quite unconscious of the great distance between the superintendent of the Dock Yard and a common workman, he had, without ceremony, seated himself. "Humph!" thought he; "I suppose that's the way they do in Russia."

"So you are from Russia, my good man?" said he, in a half-patronizing tone.

The visitor inclined his head in the affirmative.

"It's a barbarous place, I've heard: the people are not half civilized; you did wisely in coming here. You must see a great difference between it and Holland?"

"Yes," said the Russian, "we have much to learn. Other nations are greatly in advance of us in many respects; but that will pass away, and Russia will take her place at the head of them all."

The superintendent shrugged his shoulders. He evidently did not believe it.

"So you wish employment?" he continued, after a pause. "What is your name?"

"Peter Timmerman," was the reply.

"Very well; you may set to work to-morrow. Your wages will be a florin a day. You may report yourself at six

54

o'clock."

Thus terminated the interview. The Russian made a bow of acknowledgment, and left the office, leaving the superintendent more puzzled than enlightened at the insight into Russian character with which he had been favored.

The next morning, at the appointed time, Peter Timmerman presented himself at the Dock Yard. He set to work with an intelligence and earnestness which evinced that he was far from being a novice, and by no means inclined to be a drone. A week had not passed before he was acknowledged to be the ablest workman in the yard.

His fellow-workmen looked upon him with a little natural curiosity, and would have been very glad of his confidence. It was soon found, however, that, although asking many questions in regard to the details of his occupation, he preserved a uniform silence respecting his own family and past life, carefully evading any inquiries which the curiosity of his companions prompted. On one occasion, when some one of them pushed it to an indiscreet extent, the eyes of the Russian blazed with anger, and he lifted the tool he had in his hand in a threatening manner; but apparently reflection came to his aid, and, lowering it, he proceeded with his work. This little incident convinced his comrades, that, whatever mystery there might be connected with his past history, it would be both useless and dangerous in them to endeavor to extort it from him. Henceforth, then, he was not troubled with inquiries, but was treated with an involuntary and perhaps unconscious deference by those with whom he was brought in daily contact.

If occasionally it might be thought that he was greater than he seemed, there was nothing to confirm this idea in his mode of life.

The florin which he daily earned was the utmost limit of his expenses. No workman lived more frugally. He had secured board and lodgings at the house of a poor widow woman, the mother of one of his companions in the yard, where he paid a small price, and lived accordingly. The whole family consisted of the mother and son. This son, who was a lively and well-looking young man of one and twenty, was, next to Peter, the most skilful workman in the yard. He worked intelligently, and did not suffer his eyes to remain idle. It was his ambition to rise from the position of a mere workman, and become a master-builder.

Perhaps one thing which contributed to heighten his ambition was the fact that the superintendent of the Dock Yard possessed, among the items of his wealth, a fair, cherry-cheeked damsel, whose beauty had set half the hearts of the young men in Amsterdam on fire. Trust me, friendly reader! young men are pretty much alike all the world over; and the current of youthful feeling is just as likely to effervesce in the Hollander, phlegmatic as he is generally supposed, as in the residents of more southern climes.

But, after all, was it not foolish in the young ship-carpenter to aspire to an object so generally admired and sought after as the Fraulein superintendent? for such she was designated, out of respect for her father's office. Perhaps it was; and yet Heinrich Dort did not think so. After all, he was the best judge in what concerned himself.

He had observed the young Fraulein's eyes wandering toward the side of the church on which he sat, and he could not mistake the object that attracted them. Whenever the maiden saw that he was returning her gaze, she always cast down her eyes; and then, of course, she looked ten-fold as beautiful in the eyes of Heinrich Dort.

After all, the eye is more eloquent than the tongue. Heinrich thought he could not mistake it in this instance. It was certainly rather singular that the two should meet in the walk one pleasant Sabbath afternoon; and no less so, perhaps, that, precisely at the moment, the Fraulein should drop a brooch which she held in her hand. Of course, she searched for it diligently in every place but the right one; and, of course, Heinrich was required, by the claims of politeness, to volunteer his assistance. The lost ornament was soon found; but Heinrich, probably fearing it might be lost again, did not leave the Fraulein, but accompanied her, by a very round-about way, to her home. Perhaps it might have been absence of mind that made them miss the direct way,—at least, so we will conjecture, since we can do nothing more.

At all events, such was the commencement of Heinrich's acquaintance with the Fraulein. They used to meet every Sabbath afternoon; and Heinrich, acknowledging his presumption all the time, ventured to confess that his whole hope of happiness rested upon her answer to a little question which he had to propose.

What that question was, I may as well leave to be surmised. The answer was conditionally favorable. The maiden intimated that no opposition need be anticipated from her, provided he should obtain her father's consent. Heinrich felt very happy until he began to consider that this qualification might prove a very formidable one; and he feared that the superintendent might think the young workman altogether an inadequate match for his daughter, whose dowry would be twenty thousand florins at the very least. But there is an old saying,—"Faint heart never won fair lady." Whether Heinrich had ever heard of this, or whether, indeed, it had ever been translated into Dutch at all, I am quite unable to say; but, at all events, he was resolved that such a prize should not pass from his hands without a struggle.

———————

Although the young workman was far from being constitutionally timid, preserving an undaunted front in the face of danger, it must be confessed that his heart beat audibly and his hand trembled perceptibly as he knocked at the door of the superintendent's office; not that there was any thing particularly suited to inspire fear in the rotund figure of that personage.

The latter perceived that the young man was disturbed. He was rather flattered to find it so, as he attributed it solely to the effect of his presence, which he privately considered not a little imposing. It was, therefore, with an approach to affability that he motioned him to be seated, and inquired, —

"Well, my good fellow, how goes business? Have you come for any instructions?"

"No, your excellency," replied Heinrich. "Business goes well enough; but it is on another subject that I wish to trouble you."

"Well, out with it, man. No parleying, — that's my way."

"You have a daughter."

"Donder and blitzen! So I always have supposed. And is it to impart this precious piece of information that you have come here?"

"No, your excellency," hesitated Heinrich; "but the fact is, that — that — in short, an attachment has sprung up between your daughter and myself; and I am here to crave your permission to marry her."

"Well, that is coming to the point with a vengeance!"

exclaimed the testy little superintendent. "And may I beg to know whether my daughter sanctioned this visit on your part?"

"She did."

"Then she has less wit than I thought for. She—the daughter of the superintendent of the royal Dock Yard of Amsterdam—to stoop to be the wife of a common workman! The girl must be out of her senses. But if she chooses it to be so, I shall not. Young man, you have been presumptuous. For once, I will pass over it; but beware of offending a second time."

The little great man made an imperious gesture of withdrawal, which Heinrich could not do otherwise than obey. He returned home in great depression, as might be anticipated of one whose dearest hopes had been crushed out. Sitting at the door, he perceived his mother's lodger and his own fellow-workman, Peter Timmerman.

The latter, contrary to his custom, opened a conversation with Heinrich, whose manner he could not avoid noticing.

"What has befallen you, comrade," he said, "that you should look so woe-begone?"

"And if I tell you," returned Heinrich, whose disappointment had made him somewhat testy, —"if I should tell you, how could you help me?"

"Perhaps not at all,—perhaps very much. At all events, it will relieve your mind to unburden it of sorrow, if any weighs upon it."

"You may be right," said Heinrich, after a pause. "At all events, it will do no harm. You must know, then, that I have been foolish enough to fall in love with the superintendent's daughter, who favors my suit. But because I am not wealthy, and am *only a workman*" (the young man emphasized the last words in a bitter tone), "her father rejects my suit."

"But how if you occupied as high a position as himself?"

"Oh! then there would be nothing to fear."

"Listen, then, in your turn. I may help you to what you seek. Did you ever hear of Russia?"

"I have," said Heinrich. "It is a great country, but a barbarous one."

"That is true; at least, it is not so far advanced as its neighbors. But, if I live to accomplish all my plans, it shall yet equal any of them."

"*You!* Who, then, are you?" exclaimed the young man, in astonishment at such language from such a source.

"*I am Peter, the reigning czar,*" said the Russian, composedly. "I could trust no one but myself to carry out a plan I had formed for supplying the chief defect of Russia,—an efficient navy. Accordingly, I have entered myself here as a common workman. I have gained what I sought; I have made myself familiar with the construction of vessels; and I shall, after a brief visit to England, return to my kingdom, and take measures to build a fleet. I have thought of you as one competent to superintend their building. You shall have a handsome salary, and I will confer upon you an order of nobility."

"Then I can marry the Fraulein superintendent after all!" And Heinrich leaped to his feet in exultation. "But how shall I thank your ex I mean your majesty, for such a load of favors?"

"By fidelity to my interests," said Peter. "But I am tired, and must go in. Whatever arrangements you make must be completed within three days. Good night."

The next morning, Heinrich paid another visit to the superintendent. When he left, at the end of half an hour, the superintendent accompanied him to the door in the excess of his affability. No more opposition was made to his suit. Heinrich Dort, the workman, was quite a different person from Heinrich Dort, general superintendent of the Russian navy.

The events which followed are known to history. Peter, with the assistance of his superintendent, laid the foundation of a flourishing marine; and the latter, through all the mutations of the Russian dynasty, succeeded in retaining the confidence of the government until Death gathered him to his fathers at a ripe old age.

OUR GABRIELLE.

When the harsh days of the winter
  Softened into early spring,
And the birds—gay, feathered songsters—
  First commenced their carolling,
Kindling in our hearts o'erflowing
  More of love than tongue can tell,
Sweeter than the breath of morning
  Came our star-eyed Gabrielle.

And our earth-worn hearts were gladdened
  As we gazed into her eyes,—
Liquid mirrors, freshly tinted
  With the hues of paradise.
Through the long days of the summer,
  Bound as with a magic spell,
Warm and warmer in our bosoms
  Grew the love of Gabrielle.

But, alas! the summer faded,
  And the autumn leaves grew sear,
And our cherished household blossom
  Faded with the fading year.
In the quiet grave we laid her;
  There, we trust, she sleepeth well;
And we hope, when life is over,
  We shall meet our Gabrielle.

THE VEILED MIRROR.

The old year was fast drawing to a close. But a few hours, and the advent of its successor would be hailed by merry shouts and joyful gratulations, mingling with the merry chime of bells ringing out a noisy welcome from church-towers and steeples.

Adam Hathaway, a wealthy merchant, sat in his counting-room, striking a balance between his gains and losses for the year which had nearly passed. From the smile that lighted up his countenance, as he drew near the end of his task, it might safely be inferred that the result proved satisfactory.

He at length threw down his pen, after footing up the last column, and exclaimed joyfully, —

"Five thousand dollars net gain in one year! That will do very well, — very well indeed. If I am as well prospered in the year to come, it will indeed be a 'happy New Year.'"

His meditations were interrupted by a knock at the door. He opened it, and saw standing before him a man of ordinary appearance, bearing under his arm something, the nature of which he could not conjecture, wrapped up in brown paper.

"Mr. Hathaway, I believe?" was the stranger's salutation.

"You are correct."

"Perhaps, if not particularly engaged, you will allow me a few minutes' conversation with you?"

"Yes, certainly," was the surprised reply; "though I am at a loss to conjecture what can have brought you here."

"You are a wealthy man, Mr. Hathaway, and every year

increases your possessions. May I ask what is your object in accumulating so much property?"

"This is a very singular question, sir," said the merchant, who began to entertain doubts as to his visitor's sanity, —"very singular. I suppose I am influenced by the same motives that actuate other men,—the necessity of providing for my physical wants, and so contributing to my happiness."

"And this contents you? But your gains are not all devoted to this purpose. This last year, for example, the overplus has amounted to five thousand dollars."

"I know not where you have gained your information," said Mr. Hathaway, in surprise. "However, you are right."

"And what do you intend to do with this?"

"You are somewhat free with your questions, sir. However, I have no objection to answering you. I shall lay it up."

"For what purpose? I need not tell you that money, in itself, is of no value. It is only the representative of value. Why, then, do you allow it to remain idle?"

"How else should I employ it? I have a comfortable house well furnished: should I purchase one more expensive? My table is well provided: should I live more luxuriously? My wardrobe is well supplied: should I dress more expensively?"

"To these questions I answer, No. But it does not follow, because you have a good house, comfortable clothing, and a well-supplied table, that others are equally well provided. Have you thought to give of your abundance to those who are needy,—to promote your own happiness by advancing that of others?"

"I must confess that this is a duty which I have neglected. But there are alms-houses and benevolent societies. There cannot be much misery that escapes their notice," said Mr. Hathaway.

"You shall judge for yourself."

The stranger commenced unwrapping the package which he carried under his arm. It was a small mirror, with a veil hanging before it. He slowly withdrew the veil, and said, "Look!"

A change passed over the surface of the mirror. Mr. Hathaway, as he looked at it intently, found that it reflected a small room, scantily furnished; while a fire flickered in the grate. A bed stood in one corner of the room, on which reposed a sick man. By the side of it sat a woman, with a thin shawl over her shoulders, busily plying her needle. An infant boy lay in a cradle not far off, which a little girl called Alice, whose wasted form and features spoke of want and privation, was rocking to sleep.

"Would you hear what they are saying?" asked the stranger.

The merchant nodded acquiescence. Immediately there came to his ear the confused noise of voices, from which he soon distinguished that of the sick man, who asked for some food.

"We have none in the house," said his wife. "But I shall soon get this work finished; and then I shall be able to get some."

The husband groaned: "Oh that I should be obliged to remain idle on a sick bed, when I might be earning money for you and the children! The doctor says, that, now the fever has gone, I need nothing but nourishing food to raise me up again. But, alas! I see no means of procuring it. Would that some rich man, out of his abundance, would supply me with but a trifle from his board! To him it would

65

be nothing; to me, every thing."

The scene vanished; and gradually another formed itself upon the surface of the mirror.

It was a small room, neatly but not expensively furnished. There were two occupants,—a man of middle age, and a youth of a bright, intellectual countenance, which at present seemed overspread with an air of dejection.

Mr. Hathaway, to his surprise, recognized in the gentleman Mark Audley, a fellow-merchant and formerly intimate friend, who, but a few months before, had failed in business, and, too honorable to defraud his creditors, had given up all his property. Since his failure, he had been reduced to accept a clerkship.

"I am sorry, Arthur," said he to his son, "very sorry, that I could not carry out my intention of entering you at college. I know your tastes have always led you to think of a professional career; but my sudden change of circumstances has placed it out of my power to gratify you. It is best for you to accept the situation which has been offered you, and enter Mr. Bellamy's store. It is a very fair situation, and will suit you as well as any."

"I believe you are right, sir," said Arthur, respectfully; "though it will be hard to resign the hopes that I have so long cherished. I met Henry Fulham to-day. He was in my class at school, and is to enter college next fall. I couldn't help envying him. How soon will Mr. Bellamy wish me to enter his store?"

"Day after to-morrow, I believe,—that is, with the beginning of the year; New Year's Day being considered a holiday."

"Very well; you may tell him that I will come at that time."

The scene vanished as before. A change passed over the surface of the mirror. Again the merchant looked, and, to his surprise, beheld the interior of his own store. A faint light was burning, by the light of which a young man, whom he recognized as Frank Durell, one of his own clerks, was reading a letter, the contents of which seemed to agitate him powerfully.

The scene was brought so near, that he could, without difficulty, trace the lines, written in a delicate, female hand, as follows: —

"MY DEAR SON,—You are not, probably, expecting to hear from me at this time. Alas that I should have such an occasion to write! At the time of your father's death, it was supposed, that, by the sacrifice of every thing, we had succeeded in liquidating all his debts. Even this consolation is now denied us. I received a call from Mr. Perry this morning, who presented for *immediate payment* a note given by your father for fifty dollars. Immediate payment! How, with a salary barely sufficient to support us, can you meet such a charge? Can any way be devised? Mr. Perry threatens, if the money is not forthcoming, to seize our furniture. He is a hard man, and I have no hopes of appeasing him. I do not know that you can do any thing to retard it; but I have thought it right to acquaint you with this new calamity.

"Your affectionate mother,

"MARY DURELL."

The young man laid down the letter with an air of depression.

"I scarcely know how to provide for this new contingency," said he, meditatively. "My salary is small; and it requires the strictest economy to meet my expenses. I might ask for an advance; but Mr. Hathaway is particular on that point, and I should but court a refusal. But to have my mother's furniture taken from the house! The whole amount would hardly cover the debt. There is one resource; but alas that I should ever think of resorting to it! I could take the money from the till, and return it when I am able. But shall I ever be able? It would be no more nor less than robbery. At all events, I will not do it to-night. Who knows but something may turn up to help us?"

The young man blew out the lamp, and left the store. The picture faded.

"I will show you another picture, somewhat different from the others: it will be the last," said the stranger.

68

The next scene represented the interior of a baker's shop. The baker—a coarse-featured man, with a hard, unprepossessing aspect—was waiting on a woman thinly clad in garments more suitable for June than December. She was purchasing two loaves of bread and a few crackers. There was another customer waiting his turn. It was a gentleman, with a pleasant smile on his face.

"Make haste!" said the baker, rudely, to the woman, who was searching for her money to pay for her purchases. "I can't stop all day; and here's a gentleman that you keep waiting."

"Oh! never mind me: I am in no hurry," the gentleman said.

"I am afraid," said the woman, in an alarmed tone, "that I have lost my money. I had it here in my pocket; but it is gone."

"Then you may return the bread. I don't sell for nothing."

"Trust me for once, sir; I will pay you in a day or two; otherwise my children must go without food to-morrow."

"Can't help that. You shouldn't have been so careless."

The woman was about turning away, when the voice of the other customer arrested her steps.

"How much money have you lost?" he inquired.

"It was but half a dollar," was the reply; "but it was of consequence to me, as I can get no more for a day or two; and how we are to live till then, Heaven knows."

"Perhaps that will help you to decide the question." And he took from his pocket a five-dollar bill, and handed it to her.

"Oh, sir!" said she, her face lighting up with gratitude,

"this is indeed generous and noble. The blessings of those you have befriended attend you!"

She remained to make a few purchases, and then, with a light heart, departed.

The last picture faded from the mirror; and the stranger, wrapping it up, simply said,—

"You have seen how much happiness a trifling sum can produce. Will you not, out of your abundance, make a similar experiment?"

The stranger disappeared; and Mr. Hathaway awoke to find his dream terminated by the chime of the New Year's bells.

"This is something more than a dream," said he, thoughtfully. "I will, at all events, take counsel of the mystic vision; and it shall not be my fault if some hearts are not made happier through my means before another sun sets."

When the merchant arose on the following morning, it was with the light heart which always accompanies the determination to do right. He was determined that the salutation of "A happy New Year" should not be with him a mere matter of lip-service.

"I believe," said he to himself, "I will go and see my old friend, Mark Audley. If his son Arthur is really desirous of going to college, what is there to prevent my bearing the expenses? I am abundantly able, and can dispose of my money in no better way."

As he walked along with this praiseworthy determination in his heart, his attention was drawn towards a little girl, who was gazing, with eager, wistful eyes, into the window of a neighboring shop, where were displayed, in tempting array, some fine oranges. He thought—nay, he was quite sure—that in her he recognized the little girl who figured in the first scene unfolded the evening before by the mysterious mirror. By way of ascertaining, he addressed her in pleasant tone: —

"Your name is Alice, — is it not?"

"Yes, sir," said she, looking up, surprised, and somewhat awed.

"And your father is sick, — is he not?"

"Yes, sir; but he is almost well now."

"I saw you were looking at the oranges in that window. Now, I will buy you a dozen, if you will let me help you carry them home."

The purchase was made; and the merchant walked along, conversing with his little conductor, who soon lost her timidity.

Arrived at the little girl's home, he found that he had not been deceived in his presentiments. It was the same room that he had seen pictured in the mirror. The sick man was tossing uneasily in bed when Alice entered.

"See, papa," said she, joyfully, — "see what nice oranges I have for you! And here is the kind gentleman who gave them to me."

The merchant, before he left the humble apartment, gave its occupants a timely donation, and made New Year's Day a day of thanksgiving.

Mr. Hathaway soon found himself at the residence of his friend Audley, who gave him a warm welcome. "This is indeed kind," said he. "The friendship that adversity cannot interrupt is really valuable."

Mr. Hathaway now introduced the object of his visit, asking, "What do you mean to do with Arthur? He was nearly ready to go to college, — was he not?"

71

"He was; and this is one of the severest trials attending my reversed circumstances, that I am compelled to disappoint his long-cherished wish of obtaining a college education."

"That must not be," said Mr. Hathaway. "If you and Arthur will consent, I will myself pay his charges through college."

"Mr. Hathaway," said Mr. Audley, in a glow of surprise and pleasure, "this offer evinces a noble generosity on your part that I shall never forget. You must let me tell Arthur the good news."

Mr. Audley summoned his son, and, pointing to Mr. Hathaway, said, "This gentleman has offered to send you to college at his own expense."

The eyes of the youth lighted up; and he grasped the hand of his benefactor, saying, simply, "Oh! if you but knew how happy you have made me!"

"I do not deserve your thanks," was the smiling reply. "I have learned that to make others happy is the most direct way to secure my own happiness."

Mr. Hathaway took his way to the store. Arrived there, he sought out Frank Durell, and requested him to step into his office, as he wished to speak to him in private.

"Your salary is five hundred dollars a year, I believe?" said he.

"Yes, sir," said Frank Durell, somewhat surprised.

"I have come to the conclusion that this is insufficient, and I shall therefore advance it two hundred dollars; and, as a part of it may not be unacceptable to you now, here are a hundred dollars that you may consider an advance."

"Sir," said Frank Durell, hardly believing his senses, "you

cannot estimate the benefit I shall derive from this generosity. My mother, who depends upon me for support, was about to be deprived of her furniture by an extortionate creditor; but this timely gift—for I must consider it so—will remove this terrible necessity. I thank you, sir, from my heart."

"You are quite welcome," said the merchant, kindly. "In future, consider me your friend; and, if you should at any time be in want of advice or assistance, do not scruple to confide in me."

"At least," said the merchant, thoughtfully, "I have done something to make this a 'happy New Year' for others. The lesson conveyed in the dream of last night shall not be thrown away upon me. I will take care that many hearts shall have cause to bless the vision of THE VEILED MIRROR."

SUMMER HOURS.

It is the year's high noon!
   The air sweet incense yields;
   And, o'er the fresh, green fields,
Bends the clear sky of June.

I leave the crowded streets,
   The hum of busy life,
   Its clamor and its strife,
To breathe thy perfumed sweets.

Oh rare and golden hours!
   The birds' melodious song
   Wave-like is borne along
Upon a strand of flowers.

I wander far away,
   Where, through the forest trees,
   Sports the cool summer breeze
In wild and wanton play.

A patriarchal elm
   Its stately front uprears,
   Which, twice a hundred years,
Has ruled this woodland realm.

I sit beneath its shade,
   And watch, with careless eye,
   The brook that babbles by
And cools the leafy glade.

In truth, I wonder not,
   That, in the ancient days,
   The temples of God's praise
Were grove and leafy grot.

The noblest ever planned,
   With quaint device and rare,
   By man, can ill compare
With this from God's own hand.

Pilgrim with wayworn feet,
  Who, treading life's dull round,
  No true repose hast found,
Come to this green retreat;—

For bird and flower and tree,
  Green field and woodland wild,
  Shall bear, with voices mild,
Sweet messages to thee.

THE PRIZE PAINTING.

I.

It was a small attic chamber in an obscure part of London. The light that entered at the open window revealed two figures,—Arthur Elliott and his young wife.

"Dear Arthur," said the latter, as she brushed back the heavy chestnut locks from his pale brow, "you must not—indeed you must not—labor so incessantly. You will injure your health,—perhaps ruin it entirely,—and then what will be left to me?"

"Mary," said the young painter, caressingly, "you are alarming yourself to no purpose. I am not weary. Besides, what were a little weariness in comparison with the great purpose I have in view? You know the exhibition will open in a fortnight; and my picture is still unfinished. Oh!" continued he, with enthusiasm, while a faint flush overspread his pale cheek, "if it could be my fortune to gain the great prize of five hundred pounds which has been offered for the best painting on exhibition, I believe I could die content!"

"Arthur!" said his wife, reproachfully.

"But better still," said the young painter, caressingly, "to live and enjoy it with you, my sweet wife! With such a start, what might I not hope for? Fame, fortune, friends, all would be mine. But it is growing late; and I have still much to do before I retire. But do not wait for me, dear Mary: I shall work the faster, if I know that you are reposing."

Arthur Elliott was the son of a clergyman in one of the midland counties of England. At the age of seventeen, he

76

had entered the office of his uncle, an attorney in London, — a hard, worldly man, wholly engrossed in business. Young Arthur, who was a boy of a sensitive and highly imaginative temperament, found little sympathy with his peculiar tastes in the musty folios over which he was expected to pore day after day, or in the deeds and legal instruments which he was called upon to engross. He devoted his leisure time to obtaining some knowledge of painting from a teacher of that art. He made so great proficiency in this department as to surprise his teacher, who exclaimed, with enthusiasm, that he was born to be an artist.

"And why should I not be?" thought Arthur to himself. "With law I am completely disgusted: I shall never make a figure at it. Why, then, should I not abandon what I so utterly detest, and pursue that which offers so much stronger attraction?"

Full of this resolution, he went to his uncle, and requested his permission to adopt it. But the scheme appeared absurd and chimerical to the man of business; and he utterly forbade Arthur's cherishing any such plans in future. This, to one of his nephew's high spirit, was more than he could bear. His place in his uncle's office was vacant the next day, and remained so. Arthur had collected his little articles of personal property, and fled to the house of his instructor, where, undetected, he pursued his studies with the utmost assiduity. His master had a daughter, a beautiful girl, whose disposition and manners were as amiable as her features were faultless. What wonder that Arthur fell in love, and that the two, with her father's consent, exchanged vows of fidelity, though both were as yet too young to think of marriage?

This, however, was hastened by an event which plunged them both in affliction. Mary's father died. She was left alone in the world, with no one but Arthur to depend upon. Arthur was just on the verge of twenty; Mary, but sixteen. Under the circumstances, however, it was thought best that they should marry. Mary's fortune was but small, her father having left nothing behind him but the materials of his art.

At first, Arthur resolved to follow in the steps of his father-in-law, but, as is too often the case, found that genius unknown is unappreciated. His income became very scanty, —hardly sufficient to supply himself and Mary with the bare necessaries of life.

It was at this stage in their fortunes that it was announced, that, at the annual exhibition of paintings, the prize already alluded to would be awarded to the most meritorious production of art. This offer fired Arthur's ambition. Why should not he, filled as he was with the inspiration of genius,—why should not he gain it? It was not impossible. He would at least try.

He selected as his subject "The Transfiguration of the Saviour." Without entering into the details of the painting, which could only be done properly by an artist, it is sufficient to say that the conception was a grand one, and the execution of a high character.

But, in the mean time, how were they to live? The painting on which Arthur was now engaged was a work of time; and it was a considerable period before he could hope to derive any pecuniary profit from it. Thus far, Mary had assisted her husband, as far as she was able, by obtaining work from the slop-shops, which amounted to a mere pittance. But they had learned to live frugally under that sternest of teachers, —Necessity.

II.

It was early in the morning of the day after that on which

our story commences. Arthur, worn out by his midnight vigils, had not yet risen. Mary was astir: she had already prepared and eaten a frugal meal; and the small table—the only one in the apartment—was covered with a white cloth, on which was spread, with as tempting an array as the nature of the food would admit, the breakfast intended for her husband.

Suddenly, there was a violent knock at the door. Mary glanced towards her husband,—who was still buried in deep sleep,—apprehensive that he might be awakened, and then went to the door and opened it.

A coarse-featured man entered.

"Good morning, Mrs. Elliott," was his salutation. "You see I have come for my week's rent. I am not likely to forget that."

"The rent!" said Mary, apprehensively. "I am sorry, Mr. Mudge; but I haven't quite got it ready. I didn't succeed in finishing the work I had on hand as soon as I anticipated; and I must ask your indulgence for a day or two."

"Oh, yes! the old story!" said the man, with a sneer. "And if I should come again in a day or two, you wouldn't have finished the work you have on hand, and would ask for a day or two more. Oh, yes! I am used to such games."

"But, Mr. Mudge, have I failed you before? and should I be likely to begin now? If you will come on Tuesday, you shall have the money, if I have to pawn some of my furniture to raise it."

Mr. Mudge was half persuaded, but still sullen. "There's your husband,—why doesn't he work? He is able to. You wouldn't find any difficulty in raising the rent, if he would do something."

"Arthur works already beyond his strength," was the

wife's slightly indignant rejoinder (for she could not bear to have any imputation cast upon *him*); "and some day we shall see what will come of it."

Just then, her husband stirred in his sleep; and Mary, hastily repeating, "Call again on Tuesday, and you shall have it," closed the door, and went to his bedside.

"They are a proud set," said Mudge to himself, as he descended the rickety staircase, which nearly caused him to stumble, — "they are a proud set; and they say pride and poverty always go together. But, if the rent isn't ready on Tuesday, their pride will be likely to meet with a fall, or my name isn't Mudge."

Perceiving that her husband still slept, the artist's wife took up her work, and began to ply her needle busily. The work she had received from the slop-shop consisted of shirts, for which she received ninepence apiece. She had taken a bundle of six, which, when completed, would amount to a little less than a crown. By great diligence, she could make three of these in two days; which would give them an income of not quite seven shillings per week. Of this sum, one half was obliged to go for the rent of the miserable room in which they lodged.

By and by, Arthur awoke from the deep sleep in which he had been plunged, and looked around him.

"It is late," said he: "the sun is already high; and I must to work."

He dressed himself hastily, and partook of the food which his wife had prepared for him.

The next day passed; and Monday afternoon brought to Mrs. Elliott the sad conviction that she had miscalculated as to the rapidity with which she could perform her work, and that she would not, after all, be prepared to meet Mr. Mudge with the rent on the day following. Knowing his unfeeling nature, she could not doubt that he would insist on their instantly vacating the apartment. This was to be avoided at all hazards. She knew her husband's high spirit; and she feared for the consequences, if Mr. Mudge should be insolent.

Full of this thought, she took a light gold chain, which in happier days her husband had presented to her, and proceeded, with reluctant step, to the pawnbroker's. It was drawing towards evening; and she hurried through the streets, scarcely daring to look to the right hand or to the left, lest she might meet with some interruption.

Solomon Fagin, a Jew, who fully sustained the reputation of his race, as an avaricious man wholly devoted to the love of gain, stood, with a cringing expression on his drawn-up features, behind the counter of his shop in David's Alley. He was trafficking, or rather seemed to have just closed a sale, with a young gentleman well dressed and of prepossessing appearance. The latter made way politely for Mary, who was too much pre-occupied to acknowledge his courtesy.

"How much will you advance me on this?" asked she, hurriedly, extending the chain, which had originally been purchased for two guineas.

Solomon looked in her face cunningly, as if to estimate, by the degree of anxiety she displayed, how little he might venture to offer.

Mary was very nervous, and exceedingly anxious to get home before it grew much darker. This probably gave her an appearance of solicitude, which the Jew attributed to destitution.

"These things ish very sheap," he at length said, — "dog-sheap: people don't want 'em. I can't offer you more than ten shillings, and shall lose on that."

The young gentleman had been an attentive spectator of this scene. He fathomed the cunning of the Jew, and, advancing to the counter, took the chain in his hands.

"Come, Solomon, this is too bad! You should offer three times as much, and you would make a good bargain then. You know, as well as I do, that that chain never cost less than two guineas. Come, come! be honest for once."

"It ish all very well," said Solomon, who did not relish the interruption, "vor young shentleman to talk; but if young shentleman should keep a pawnbroker's shop, he would change his mind."

"Perhaps so; but I will wait till I am a pawnbroker first. But, Solomon, if you don't offer more, I'll take it myself."

The Jew, who was afraid of losing a good bargain, and internally cursing the interference of the young gentleman, began to mumble that it was very hard to press a poor man so,—that he should certainly lose on it. However, he closed by offering fifteen shillings.

Mrs. Elliott was about to close with this offer; but the other stepped forward, and said,—

"No, no! this will never do. That chain cost two guineas at least. I am sure of it; for I bought one precisely similar the other day. Give it to me, madam," said he, respectfully, to Mrs. Elliott, "and I will advance you that sum."

The artist's wife accepted his proffer with grateful astonishment, and hastened to leave the shop. She had gone but a few steps, when she was overtaken by the chance companion whom she had met at the pawnbroker's.

"Do not think me bold," said he, "if I suggest that it is hardly safe to carry money open in your hand; and, indeed, it is so dark, that it is hardly safe at all for a lady to pass through the streets unattended. If you will accept my escort,

I shall be most happy to conduct you to your lodgings."

Mrs. Elliott hesitated. She knew it was scarcely safe to trust to an entire stranger; but the young man's conduct thus far had so prepossessed her in his favor, that she did not refuse.

"Sir," she replied, after a moment's hesitation, "I know not whether I am in the right; but I cannot help trusting you. I do not think you intend to impose upon me. I *will* trust to you."

"You shall not regret your confidence," said her companion. "May I ask where you reside?"

"At 16, S Street," was the reply of Mrs. Elliott. "I am much indebted to you, sir, no less for the trouble you are now taking than for the generosity with which you saved me from being imposed upon by the Jew."

"Oh!" said the other, laughing, "Solomon is a cunning old fellow, who will cheat where he gets a chance. No worse Jew for that, or pawnbroker either. It is their business to cheat; and I fancy Fagin is as much of an adept at it as any one.

"I hope," he continued, after a pause, "that you were not driven by distress to the sale of an article which you must value highly?"

"It was presented to me by my husband," was the reply. "I would not have parted with it, but that this was probably the only means of saving ourselves from being turned out of doors."

"I am sorry for that," was the sympathizing reply. "Does your husband know that you have come out on such an errand?"

"No, or he would have offered to pawn some of his own clothing first. Of this I was afraid; and it was for this reason that I stole secretly out."

They had now reached the outer door of the dwelling in the upper part of which Mr. Elliott lodged. It was necessary for them to part.

In parting, the stranger pressed Mrs. Elliott's hand, and then walked rapidly away. She found, to her astonishment, that he had placed the chain in her hand. But he was now so far distant that she could not call him back. Thanking him in her heart for this unlooked-for generosity, Mrs. Elliott went up stairs with a light heart; for she foresaw, that, with the sum of money of which she had so providentially come into possession, they would be able to live comfortably for some weeks; in addition to which, she would have it in her power to procure some delicacies for her husband's palate.

After a little consideration, she decided not to mention this adventure to her husband; as the idea of her selling his gift would be painful to him, and would do him no good. There was no danger of his inquiring, so much was he absorbed in his painting. Besides, if he thought at all upon the subject, he would think she had been out on business connected with her work.

She hastily passed up stairs, and set about preparing supper for herself and husband.

III.

The sun was not more punctual to his hour of rising than was the visit of Mr. Mudge, the landlord, to the lodging of the artist.

"Well," said he, abruptly, "have you got the rent ready? I can't wait a day longer."

"Nor will it be necessary," said Mrs. Elliott, calmly. "Here is the money."

Mr. Mudge, notwithstanding his love of money, looked a little disappointed at this ready payment. His mind was essentially a vulgar one; and he felt an instinctive aversion to Mrs. Elliott, whose superiority to himself he could not help admitting. He had hoped to have the pleasure of turning them out.

"Well, they won't always have ready money," was his internal reflection; "and, the first good excuse I have, they shall go, bag and baggage."

Meanwhile, Mr. Elliott was making progress on his painting.

"You deserve the prize, Arthur," said his wife, after gazing admiringly upon her husband's work, — "you deserve it; and I hope that you will be successful in obtaining it."

"It has cost me many hours of hard labor," said the artist, wearily, as he laid aside his pallet for a moment, and passed his hand across his brow. "I never felt so great an interest in a picture before; and now two days' labor, I think, will complete it. It needs but a few touches."

As he spoke, Mary saw an unnatural flush upon his cheek, and that his eye glowed with an unusual brilliancy. She was alarmed.

"Do, Arthur, for my sake, lie down and rest a while. You do not look well, and sleep will refresh you. You say two days will finish it, and you have a week before you."

"I believe I will lie down for a few minutes," said Arthur; "for my head aches strangely, and I feel weary."

He laid down; but it did not refresh him. In a little while, he became feverish, so that he could not leave his bed. His wife went out to summon a physician. All her hopes centred in Arthur; and the thought that he was sick, that he was in danger, quickened her step. She saw nothing that was going on around her, so intent was she on her object, till suddenly some one touched her familiarly on the shoulder. She looked around, and saw by her side the companion whom she had encountered at the pawnbroker's.

"I am happy to meet you once more," said he; "but you seem in haste."

"Yes," said she, hurriedly; "my husband has been suddenly taken sick, and I am in pursuit of a physician."

"Let me relieve you of that duty. If you will return to your husband, who doubtless needs your presence, I will summon a physician. I know your lodgings, and will return with medical assistance immediately."

Mrs. Elliott gratefully accepted this proffer of service, for she had felt much solicitude. When she returned, she found her husband seized with a fit of delirium, in which he uttered incoherent sentences, all of which had some connection with his picture and the approaching exhibition.

In a few minutes, the stranger returned with a physician. To the anxious inquiries of Mrs. Elliott, the doctor replied, —

"Your husband is suffering from the excitement and fatigue consequent upon too severe mental exertion. This has thrown him into a fever, from which it will take time to recover."

After leaving directions, he withdrew, promising to repeat his visit the next day.

"How much my poor husband will be disappointed!" Mrs. Elliott could not help exclaiming. "He must now abandon the hope of presenting his picture at the exhibition."

"What!" said her visitor, with interest, "is your husband an artist?"

In reply, Mrs. Elliott led him to a corner of the room, and withdrew the screen that concealed the painting.

He gazed upon it with deep admiration for some minutes, and then said, with enthusiasm, —

"Ah! this is indeed beautiful!"

"It is nearly completed," said the artist's wife; "but that will be of no service to us now." And she let fall the screen, and sighed heavily.

A sudden idea struck the visitor.

"Will you trust the painting to me for a few days?" he asked. "You shall not regret it."

Mrs. Elliott, convinced that her husband would not recover in time to finish it, assented without difficulty. She never thought of distrusting one who had been of such essential service.

"Thank you," said the visitor. "As you have reposed this confidence in me, I must acquaint you with my name and address, that you may know whom you have trusted."

He handed her a card containing the following direction: "F. Sedley, 7, Covent Place."

"I will send for it this afternoon," said he, as he withdrew, "and will call in upon you again to-day or to-morrow. I shall be anxious to learn how your husband gets on."

The delirium which attended the early stages of Mr. Elliott's indisposition continued for some days. At length, consciousness returned.

"How long have I been sick?" he inquired.

He was told.

"And what day is it now?"

"Wednesday, the fourteenth."

"And to-morrow the exhibition will take place. Oh that I could have held out but two days longer! I would have asked for no more. In that time I should have completed my painting, and it would have been entered in competition. Fate seems to be against me."

He groaned, and covered his face with his hands.

"But," said his wife, soothingly, "remember, dear Arthur, that, if Fate seems against us, God is always with us. He orders every thing in infinite wisdom."

"But," was the hardly reconciled answer, "his ways are very difficult of comprehension. The wisdom is hidden. I cannot see it."

"Yet," said his wife, full of hopeful confidence, "if we trust in him, we shall not be deceived."

"But," said Arthur, after a pause, "how shall we live in the mean time? I can do nothing now for our support; and much of your time is taken up in attendance upon me."

"I am richer than you think," said Mary, opening her purse, and displaying the sum she had received from her visitor, much of which was still untouched.

To his inquiries how she obtained it, she replied by unfolding the whole story, and indulged in the warmest encomiums on the generosity and kindness of Mr. Sedley, whose providential interposition had saved her from being imposed upon by the avaricious pawnbroker. Arthur was interested in the recital, and expressed a wish to become acquainted with him. After a pause, he inquired for the painting. "Let me look upon it once more," said he. "Perhaps I shall be better able to judge of its merits after a lapse of time."

Mary looked embarrassed. "Excuse me," said she to her husband; "but Mr. Sedley expressed a wish to carry it home with him for a few days, and I could not refuse. Doubtless he wished to exhibit it to some of his friends; and in that way it may find a purchaser."

Arthur acquiesced in this conclusion, and approved of the course which Mary had adopted.

IV.

It was the morning of the exhibition,—a clear, bright morning in September, which seemed to combine all the balmy softness of summer with a freedom from its excessive heat. The sun shone down upon the numberless roofs of the great city, and found its way into the lanes and alleys, lighting them up, for the hour, with a brightness not their own. Through the little window—the only one—by which light was admitted into the room where the Elliotts lodged, the golden rays streamed in, and lent their glory to the face of the sleeping artist, who had not yet awakened from the night's slumber.

There was a knock at the door. Mary opened it; and Mr. Sedley made his appearance.

"To-day," said he, "is the day of the exhibition. Will you accompany me? I have a free pass."

"But my husband?" said she, doubtfully. "I cannot leave him."

"I have provided for that. I have brought a nurse with me, who will take your place, and remain here with your husband. She is skilful and experienced, and you can safely trust him in her hands."

Here the sleeper awoke, and Mary introduced Mr. Sedley to her husband. The latter thanked him warmly for the interest he had manifested in their welfare, and insisted on Mary's accompanying him to the exhibition.

"Though I shall have no part in it," he said, "I still wish to hear all about it."

Mary could no longer refuse, but, dressing herself as neatly as her limited wardrobe would admit, prepared to accompany Mr. Sedley. To her surprise, she found a private carriage waiting, with the usual accompaniments of a coachman and a footman; the latter of whom very deferentially opened the door of the carriage, and waited for her to enter.

She began to entertain new ideas of her companion's consequence. The carriage dashed boldly through the narrow streets, until it emerged from them into the more fashionable and crowded thoroughfares.

Mary found sufficient to amuse her in the splendid carriages, many of them surmounted with a coronet, all hastening in the same direction with themselves. There was an unusual number in the streets,—a circumstance which was easily explained by the interest and curiosity which had been awakened by the exhibition.

At length, they reached the magnificent hall in which it was to be held. The porter bowed deferentially to Mr. Sedley as he made way for him to pass.

And now they are in the room. What a magnificent collection! It represented the combined genius of the British artists, nearly all of whom had contributed to it. Mary, who, though no artist, had caught something of the spirit from her husband, looked about her in speechless admiration.

"This is indeed grand!" said she, at last. "It surpasses my highest expectations."

"It is indeed," said Mr. Sedley. "England has good cause to be proud of her artists. But see! do you not recognize an old acquaintance?"

Mary looked, and, to her unbounded surprise, beheld "The Transfiguration of Christ"—her husband's painting—suspended against the wall. Mr. Sedley hastened to explain.

"I thought it a pity," he said, "that so fine a picture should be lost to the exhibition. I accordingly hired an artist to give it the last touches, and had it brought here."

Mary thanked him with a glance full of gratitude. She looked again, and beheld her husband's picture surrounded by eager admirers. Among them were the titled and noble; and it was with an emotion of pride that she heard the expressions of admiration which it elicited, and the eager questionings as to the author's name.

"I do not know," she heard one say: "I believe it is some *protégé* of Sir Francis Sedley. At all events, he presented it."

"Sir Francis Sedley?" she inquired, pausing, and looking in her companion's face.

"I cannot deny it," said he, smiling. "But come: let us draw nearer to the head of the hall: the prizes are to be announced."

They pressed forward; and the chairman of the committee arose, and after a few preliminary remarks, in which he commented on the difficulty they had experienced in making the award, and congratulated himself on the splendid collection which had that day been brought together, announced that the first prize, of five hundred pounds, was awarded to Arthur Elliott for his painting entitled "The Transfiguration."

Loud shouts rang through the hall.

Mary was oppressed by the fulness of her joy.

"Let me go out into the air,—I shall feel relieved," she said.

91

Sir Francis kindly accompanied her.

"Oh, sir!" said she, "it is to you that we are indebted for this great joy. Poor Arthur! how he will be delighted!"

"Will you not return to him and communicate it?" asked Sir Francis.

A hackney coach was called, and Mrs. Elliott soon arrived at her lodgings.

"Oh, Arthur!" said she. "The prize! the prize!" It was all that she could utter.

"Who has got it?" asked the sick man, eagerly, as he rose in his bed.

"It is yours! They have awarded it to you!"

A proud flush passed over the faint cheek of the artist. "I am satisfied,—I am happy," said he.

The joy occasioned by his success operated most beneficially on the sunken energies of the artist. Before many weeks, he recovered fully, so as to resume his art. His prize painting was sold for a great sum to an English nobleman, who was bent on adding it to his collection.

———————

At present, there is a beautiful cottage situated a few miles out of London, in the suburbs. There is a pleasant garden connected with it, and it seems the abode of peace and happiness. This is the residence of the eminent artist, Arthur Elliott, and his happy wife. There are few households to whom it has fallen to enjoy such unalloyed happiness as theirs. They have not forgotten the author of their prosperity. In the library of Sir Francis Sedley there hangs a beautiful picture,—a perfect gem of art,—on the back of which is traced, in delicate characters,—

"Arthur Elliott to his Benefactor."

THE CHILD OF THE STREET.

Through the silent thoroughfares
    Of a city rich and great,
Shivering in the pitiless blast,
    Walked a poor child, desolate.

Bright and cold the stars looked down,
    Glittering in a field of blue;
But they brought no warmth to her
    Whom the winds pierced through and through.

Hugging tight her ragged shawl,
    On she hies with hurried feet,
Gliding like a phantom form
    Through the darkness-shrouded street.

Cheerful homes are very near;
    Happy firesides hem her in;
And she hears from many a window
    Careless childhood's merry din.

No warm fireside her awaiteth;
    On no couch her limbs shall lie:
For the cold street is *her* dwelling;
    And *her* chamber's roof, the sky.

Fiercely blows the northern blast,
    Penetrating every fold
Of her thin shawl; and she whispers,
    Shivering, "I am very cold!"

Hark! the bells with brazen clangor,
    Rising every moment higher,
Peal upon the startled city
    The terrific cry of "Fire!"

O'er the child's face, wan and weary,
    Comes a quick flush of delight,
As she marks a lofty steeple
    Wreathed in spires of lurid light.

Onward with the hurrying crowd
    Pressed the child through wind and storm,
With one thought to cheer her bosom, —
    She would once again be warm.

Once again! Through every fibre
   Creeps a warm, reviving glow,
As with outstretched hands the maiden
   Standeth in the street below.

Little reck the gallant firemen,
   As their saving task they ply,
Of the poor child who is standing
   Where the burning cinders lie.

"Stand from under! stand from under!"
   Rises high the voice of all,
As the swaying steeple totters,
   Slowly totters, to its fall.

One there was that did not heed it,
   One there was that did not stir,
Till too late! The blazing rafters
   In their fall enveloped *her*.

Child of want and heir of sorrow,
   Chill and famished, weak and faint,
Thou hast passed from out the shadow;
   Thou *no more* art desolate.

LOST AND FOUND.

I.

We are apt to look to the Old World exclusively for
startling contrasts between fashion and splendor on the one
hand, and squalid wretchedness and crime on the other.
With an air of complacency, we speak of our great and
happy republic, as affording a retreat for the homeless, and a
refuge for the oppressed. Yet, in the face of all this, it would
be difficult to find in any European city a more thoroughly
vicious district than that of the Five Points in New York.
Few, doubtless, of the fashionable crowds who daily
promenade Broadway, have ever penetrated its recesses, —
few but would shrink in dismay from horrors of which they
had not even dreamed, if they should do so. But it is not
our purpose to moralize upon that which has already
begun to attract the attention, and inspire the exertions, of
philanthropic hearts and hands. That task we leave to abler
pens. Enough that we have hinted at the character of the
locality in which our story takes its rise.

One of the worst recesses of this notorious district enjoys
the singularly euphonious name of "Cow Bay." The
entrance to it is a filthy arched passage-way, round which
are crowded miserable tenements; so miserable, that the
scanty sunlight, which finds its way through the dirt-
begrimed windows, seems to shrink away, as if it were more
than half ashamed of the company it is in. In front of these
houses, you may see men whose faces betray no evidence of
intelligence or virtue; women whose miserable and woe-
begone expression, perchance loud voice and angry
vituperation, attest that from them all that renders the sex
attractive has for ever departed; children—and this is the

97

saddest sight of all—dirty and sickly, and who are children only in size and in years; for upon their hearts the happy influences of genuine childhood have never fallen. For them, alas! life is a rough pathway, paved with flinty stones, which pierce their feet at every step.

A tall man, with a shambling gait, and hat drawn over his eyes, walked swiftly through the arched passage-way above alluded to, and, muttering an imprecation upon a child who got in his way, entered one of the houses, whose front door stood invitingly open, and, groping his way up the staircase, which was quite obscure, although it was mid-day, opened a door at the head of the staircase, and entered.

It was such a room as the appearance of the house might lead one to expect. It was, however, furnished more ambitiously; as at least one-half the floor was covered with a rag carpet, and the scanty furniture was arranged with rather more taste than might have been anticipated. By the window sat a girl of twelve, sewing. Between her and the children who were playing outside there was a wide contrast. She was perfectly clean and neat in her attire; and her face, though pale,—as it might well be, shut up as she was in a noisome quarter of a great city, with no chance to breathe the fresh country air, or roam at will through green fields,—was unusually winning and attractive.

The man we have referred to threw himself with an air of weariness on a chair near the door, and muttered ungraciously,—

"Why haven't you got dinner ready? I'm hungry."

"Is it time?" asked the child, springing from her seat quickly, as if afraid of having neglected her duty.

"Time enough," returned the man; "for I've been at work this morning, and have got an appetite like a wolf. Besides, I want you to be through soon; for I shall send you out shopping this afternoon. Has any one been in to see me this forenoon, Helen?"

"No," said Helen (for that was her name).

"Good. I don't care to have visitors."

Helen quickly brought out, from a closet hard by, a plate of cold meat, some cold vegetables, and a plate of bread and butter. The man drew his chair to the table, and during the next quarter of an hour, in which he was so busily occupied with satisfying his appetite that he had no time for any thing else, said not a word to the child, who, on her part, was too much accustomed to his manner to utter a word.

At length, having accomplished his task in a manner so satisfactory that very little remained on the table, he drew his chair away, and motioned the child to take her place at it.

"Take your place and eat, Helen," said he, a little less gruffly than before; "and, while you are eating, I will tell you of a little plan I have formed for you."

"How do you like living here?" he resumed when she had seated herself.

She looked into his face, as if to know whether it would do to express her real opinion. His face was not so forbidding as it appeared at times, and she ventured to say, —

"I—I think there are some places which I should like better."

"No doubt, no doubt, Helen. I think I have known pleasanter places myself. But where do you think you should like to live best; that is, supposing you could live wherever you chose?"

"Oh!" said the child, her eyes brightening, and her whole

face glowing with excitement, "I should like, above all things, to live in the country, where I could run about the fields, and hear the birds sing, and—and Oh! the country is so beautiful! I think I lived there once,—did I not, uncle?"

"Yes, Helen; but it is a good while ago. How would you like to live there once more?"

"May I? Can I? Will you let me?" asked the child, eagerly.

"Perhaps so. But it will depend on whether you will be good, and try to please me."

"Oh! I will do whatever you say."

"Well, that sounds well. Then I'll tell you what my plans are, and where it is that you are to go."

So saying, he drew from his pocket a copy of the "New York Tribune," and read aloud the following advertisement:
—

> "WANTED, by a family a few miles distant from the city, a young girl, of from twelve to fourteen, to serve as nursery-maid and companion for two young children. Address
>
> "P. H. GREGORY."

"There," said the reader, laying down his paper, "is a situation which will just suit you. You like children; and pretty much all you will have to do will be to attend to them. Then Mr. Gregory lives in a beautiful place. He is a rich man, and can afford it. Would you like to go?"

"Above all things," said Helen, eagerly (for to her the prospect of a release from the dismal place in which she lived was most pleasing).

"And you wouldn't miss me, your affectionate uncle?" said the man, with a peculiar expression.

The child's eyes fell. She blamed herself frequently for not

100

holding in higher regard the only relative of whom she knew any thing: yet so ungenial was his nature, and so harsh and forbidding was he nearly always, that it would have been singular if he had inspired affection in any one. So it happened, that, in the joy of the anticipated change, she had not for a moment thought of the separation which it must occasion between herself and her uncle.

"Of course," she said, timidly, "I shall be sorry to leave you"——

"You needn't say any thing more, child," was the reply. "I don't profess any particular affection for you, and I don't believe you feel any for me; and you may be sure I shouldn't have proposed this removal to you if I had not some object of my own in it. Would you like to know what that is?"

"Yes," she said, hesitatingly.

"Well, I will tell you; because it is necessary that you should fully understand, before you go, on what conditions I allow you to do so. But, if you dare to impart to a breathing soul a hint of what I tell you, I will seek you out, and—well, no matter," he continued, seeing that his threat made her turn pale. "You must know that this Mr. Gregory, with whom I am going to place you, once cheated me out of a large sum of money, which I cannot hope to regain, except by stratagem. Now, I want you to get in there, and I will then give you instructions how to manage. They keep a large amount of valuable plate in the lower part of the house. It will be comparatively easy for you, when you are once there, to render me essential service by opening the front door to me, so that I may be able to secure it without detection; and then"——

"But," said the girl, shrinking in dismay from this proposition, "would not that be robbery?"

"Robbery? Pooh, child! Didn't I tell you that he had

cheated me out of twice the value of the plate? And, as I can't get my pay in any other way, it's perfectly proper to get it in that."

Helen was no casuist. She had never had any one to teach her right principles; but she had an instinctive feeling that this was wrong. She wished to remonstrate, but dared not. Her uncle saw her embarrassment, and guessed its cause. He rose from his seat, and stood sternly confronting her.

"Helen Armstrong," said he, in a compressed voice, "unless you promise me faithfully to perform the part I have assigned you, I will bind you out to Brady Tim, the grocer."

This Brady Tim was a repulsive character, and kept a grocery of the lowest kind nearly opposite the rooms occupied by the girl and her uncle. He was a complete tyrant, and would often beat his children in the most unmerciful manner. Their shrieks, which she was often doomed to hear, would always make her blood run cold, and inspired her with an inconceivable dread of the man who occasioned them. This her uncle well understood; and he was well aware that no threat which he could utter would make so deep an impression upon the child's mind.

"You have your choice," said he. "Shall I tell Brady Tim that you will come to-morrow morning? or will you go to Mr. Gregory's?"

"I will go," said the child, overawed.

"And you will follow my directions?"

"Yes."

"Then preparations must instantly be made. I shall have to buy you a few things to have you go looking decently. Have you got a good bonnet?"

"Only my old one, and that is bent every way."

"Well, I will get you a new one. You will also want a shawl and some gloves. As you are to be a companion to the children, it will be a recommendation if you go looking neat and comfortable. It won't take long to purchase them; and whatever else you need I can send you afterwards. Wait a moment, and I will be ready to accompany you."

He went into the inner room, and quickly emerged, completely metamorphosed in his personal appearance by a white wig and whiskers, and a staff, on which he leaned heavily. The girl looked at him in astonishment.

"What sort of a grandfather do you think I shall make?" said he, laughing. "I shall go out with you to Mr. Gregory's; and I have no doubt, that, in consideration of my gray hairs, they will be induced to take my grand-daughter into their service."

So saying, he left the room, accompanied by the child, who had improved the interval in smoothing her hair, over which she placed an ugly straw bonnet, which, however, was shortly to be displaced by one of a prettier pattern. Their purchases completed, they stepped into an omnibus, which would convey them within half a mile of Mr. Gregory's.

II.

A few miles distant from the city was a tasteful brown cottage, having a piazza on all sides, and surrounded by a carefully trained hedge. This was the summer retreat of P. H. Gregory, a New York merchant.

It was a warm day in June. Two children, a boy and girl, respectively of six and eight years, were playing in the yard, when they espied through the hedge an old man, with hair and whiskers white as the driven snow, accompanied by a young girl, toiling, apparently with great difficulty, towards the house, notwithstanding the assistance he derived from a stout cane, on which he leaned heavily.

Attracted by the sight, they ran into the house, calling on their mother to look out and see. She had scarcely done so, when, to her surprise, she found that the pair had entered the gate, and were coming towards the house.

"Is Mrs. Gregory within?" asked the old man of the servant who answered the bell.

Mrs. Gregory anticipated the reply by coming forward.

"Poor old man!" said she, compassionately (for the attire which Armstrong had donned for the occasion was singularly threadbare, and evinced the lowest depth of destitution), — "poor old man! what can I do for you?"

"I have brought my grand-daughter with me, good lady," said the old man, feebly, "in answer to your advertisement. She's a good girl, and I wish I could keep her with me; but the times are hard, and it costs a sight to live; and so I've been thinking the best thing I could do is to get her a good place, and a good mistress, as I am sure you would be to her, madam."

Mrs. Gregory's sympathies were enlisted in the child's favor by this artful address, as well as by her own modest and downcast look. She was not aware, however, that not a little of her confusion arose from the dissimulation in which she was compelled to take a part.

"What is your grand-daughter's name?" asked Mrs. Gregory. "She seems young."

"She is only twelve; but she's capable, — very capable. When her poor grandmother was sick for nearly a year before she died," — and Armstrong wiped his eyes with his ragged sleeve at the sorrowful thought, — "Helen took the whole care of her and of me; and no one could find a better nurse."

"It must have been a great care to you, Helen," said Mrs. Gregory, kindly.

Helen had been so much taken aback by the last fabrication respecting a grandmother of whom she had never heard, that she was barely able to say, in a low voice, —

"Yes, ma'am."

"But you will never regret it, my child," said the lady. "God will not fail to reward good children. So your name is Helen?"

"Yes, ma'am."

"I like the name. I had a child of that name once. Were she living, she would be about your age. But"—and the lady sighed deeply—"she disappeared one day, and we never could find any trace of her."

Had Mrs. Gregory been an attentive observer, she would have seen a gleam of intelligence pass over the old man's face at this moment; but she was too much absorbed by her sad thoughts.

"I think," said she, after a pause, "that I will engage you, Helen, although you are rather young for my purpose. When can you come?"

"She is ready now," said her grandfather. "I can send her the rest of her clothes."

"Very well. Then you may come in, and take off your things."

"Come, Helen, and give a parting kiss to your poor old grandfather. He will be very lonely without you, my dear child; but he knows that he has left you with a kind lady, who will care for you."

105

Helen advanced to her grandfather's embrace with very little alacrity. As he pressed his lips lightly to her cheek, he whispered, so that she only could hear, —

"Keep your eyes open;" and then added aloud, "Be a good girl, Helen, and mind the kind lady who has engaged you, in all respects. Remember all the lessons I have taught you; and do not forget," he continued, with a meaning look, "what I told you before I came away."

Helen replied faintly in the affirmative. Mrs. Gregory attributed her evident embarrassment to the fact that she was about to leave her only relative to go among strangers; and she resolved in her heart to lighten, as well as she might, the sorrow of the child.

"I will bring your clothes to-morrow, my dear grand-daughter," said Armstrong, as he rose slowly from his chair, and, resuming his cane, walked feebly from the house.

As soon, however, as he was fully out of sight, he straightened his bowed form, and walked rapidly onward till overtaken by a passing omnibus, which he entered, and was soon carried back to the city.

III.

Helen was not long in making the acquaintance of Ellen and Frank Gregory, the children of her employer, over whom she was expected thenceforth to have oversight.

Those who have always lived in the country, or to whom frequent visits have made it familiar, can hardly appreciate the depth of enjoyment which it brought to a child, who, like Helen, had been confined for years in the most noisome portion of a great city. To her, the most common objects seemed invested with an interest altogether new; and she plucked with as much eagerness the dandelions and buttercups which covered the greensward in profusion as if they had been the rarest exotics. There is a freemasonry in children which does away with formal introductions and the barriers of etiquette. When, two hours after her companion's departure, Helen and the children came bounding in, flushed with exercise, Mrs. Gregory had an opportunity to observe—what before had escaped her notice—that Helen was more than ordinarily pretty. Something there was in her expression that seemed to strike the chords of memory; but Mrs. Gregory dismissed it as only a chance resemblance.

"Helen," said she, calling the child to her side, "have you always lived in the city?"

"For a long time, madam. I cannot remember ever to have lived anywhere else."

"And do you like it as well as the country?"

"I do not like it at all,—it is so dark and dirty and close. The sun does not shine there as it does here; and I could not run out into the fields, but all day long I had to sit alone."

"Alone? Wasn't your grandfather with you?"

"Yes," said Helen, casting down her eyes. "He would come home to meals; but he had to attend to his business."

"He seems too old and infirm to be able to do much," said Mrs. Gregory, compassionately.

Helen was about to disclaim the age and infirmity, when the thought of the near relation in which Armstrong stood to her came over her mind in time, and she only answered, "Yes, ma'am."

"How long since your grandmother died?"

This, too, was an embarrassing question for Helen; but the necessity of saying something prompted her to reply, "A good while."

Perceiving, though she could not conjecture why, that her questions confused Helen, Mrs. Gregory desisted.

It was about four o'clock on the succeeding afternoon that Mrs. Gregory, who was sitting at the window, detected the bent form of the assumed old man slowly making his way up the hill.

"Your grandfather is coming," said she to Helen, who sat beside her.

Helen tried to look as joyful as the approach of her only relative might be expected to make her; but the thought of the deception which she was even then practising towards a family who were showing her great kindness, and the still greater wrong which she was required to do them, made it a difficult task for one no better versed in dissimulation.

Mrs. Gregory noticed it no further than to form the opinion that she was a little odd in her manners.

As Helen expected, Armstrong requested her to walk a little apart with him; and then, dropping at once the whining tone he had assumed, inquired, quickly and peremptorily, —

"Well, what have you discovered?"

"Nothing," said Helen, timidly, and as if deprecating his anger.

"Nothing?" he echoed, his eyes lighting with indignation. "What am I to understand by that?

"Come, child," said he, softening his tone, as he saw that she was terrified by his roughness, "I don't mean you any harm; but the fact is, I have placed you here to help me, and help me you must, otherwise I shall be compelled to carry you back to live with me in New York. Perhaps you would like to go?"

"Oh, no, no!" said Helen. "Don't carry me back! Let me stay here!"

"Well, so I will, if you behave well. Now, tell me truly, have you no idea where they keep the silver? I know they have a large quantity of it."

Helen reluctantly admitted, that, although she did not know, she could form an idea.

"Where?" asked Armstrong, eagerly.

"In the pantry, at the west corner of the house."

"Humph! And do they lock the door at night?"

"Yes; but the key remains in the lock."

"So far, so good. Does any one sleep in the lower part of the house?"

"No one."

"Better still."

A moment afterwards, Armstrong added, a new thought striking him, —

"I have not seen any dog near the house. Do they keep any?"

"No."

"That is lucky. A determined dog is sometimes a troublesome customer. I recollect, one night, Dick Hargrave and I had planned a little expedition of this kind, when it was all broken up by a cursed bull-dog, who rushed out upon us as if he would tear us to pieces; and, to tell the truth, he did tear Dick's coat off his back."

Helen listened in dismay; for it revealed to her what she had not known, — that her uncle had been implicated in affairs of a similar kind before. It will be remembered that Armstrong, in proposing to her to co-operate with him, had used the pretext that Mr. Gregory had cheated him, and that he was resolved to repay himself. This, Helen had believed at the time; but his present unguarded remarks led her to entertain strong doubts of its truth. Her strong natural dislike for the duplicity and treachery required at her hands determined her, in spite of her habitual timidity and fear of her companion, to venture a remonstrance. This, however, she delayed till he should make a specific demand upon her.

He resumed: "I don't know but there's a pretty good chance of success. To-night is Tuesday night. I can't very well get ready before Friday. On that night, you must contrive, in some manner,—taking care to incur no suspicion,—to come down stairs and unlock the front door. I shall be on hand at one o'clock. Be very particular about the time; for what I do must be done quickly."

"But, uncle, wouldn't that be robbery?"

"Robbery! Didn't I tell you that old Gregory had cheated me out of more than the sum I shall take?"

"But they have treated me kindly; and it makes me feel ashamed to know that I am trying to injure them, uncle" — —

"Don't call me uncle again! I'm no uncle of yours," said Armstrong, roughly. Noticing the child's look of surprise, he added, "There, the murder is out! I had intended to treat you as a niece; but you don't deserve it. It is time to talk to you in a different strain. I declare to you, Helen, that, unless you comply with my command, I will make you repent it most bitterly. Do you hear?"

"Yes," said Helen, terrified no less by his looks than his words.

"Then take care that you remember: Friday night, at one. And now, as we understand each other, that is all that is necessary."

They returned to the house in silence. Armstrong, with a hypocritical whine, thanked Mrs. Gregory for her kindness to his dear grand-daughter, who, he was glad to find, seemed so contented and happy in her new position.

"You will pardon an old man's tears," said he, drawing his hand across his eyes; "but she is all that is left to me now."

"What a good old man!" thought Mrs. Gregory, as she hastened to assure him that whatever she could do to add to the comfort of his grand-daughter would cheerfully be done.

As for Helen, she was astonished and confused at what she had discovered. She had always been led to believe that Armstrong was her uncle, and had more than once reproached herself for the dislike she could not help entertaining for him. Now he had himself disclaimed the relationship; and Helen was left to conjecture fruitlessly who and what she was.

IV.

We must carry the reader back some nine or ten years. In front of a pleasant country residence, a child of three years sat on the grass, plucking the flowers that grew at her feet, and then tossing them from her. Ever and anon she would utter a cry of childish delight, as a gaudily-painted butterfly flew past her, and would stretch out her little hands to arrest its flight; but the wanderer of the air found no difficulty in eluding the tiny hands of the child.

At length, as if weary of her pastime, she rose from her

grassy seat, and tottled towards the open gate, out of which she passed, and strayed along the path by the roadside, pausing where fancy prompted. Her disappearance had not been noted by those in the house, partly because their attention was occupied by a tall, swarthy woman, with fierce black eyes, who was at that moment asking, or rather demanding, alms of the mistress of the house.

"We are not in the habit," said the latter, "of giving money; but whatever food you may require will be cheerfully given."

"I don't want any food," said the woman, abruptly. "You talk as if victuals was the only thing one could need. I have had something to eat already. I want money, I tell you."

"Then why don't you work for it?" asked the lady, somewhat offended at the boldness of her speech.

"Because I don't see why I should work my life out while others are living in plenty. There are plenty of fine ladies who wouldn't lift their fingers if it was to save a life. Am I not as good as they? Why, then, should they fare any better than I?"

"That I do not pretend to say. I only know that he is most happy who strives to content himself with that station in which the Almighty has placed him."

"Oh! it is all very well for those to talk of being contented who have every thing to make them so. Very praiseworthy it is, to be sure!" said the woman, laughing scornfully.

The violence of her language increased to such an extent, that Mrs. Gregory—for it was she—found it necessary to order her to leave the house. She did so, but not without many imprecations. As she strode along with hasty steps, she espied by the roadside a little girl, holding in her hand a flower that she had just plucked.

"Isn't it *pitty*?" said the child, holding it up.

A thought struck the woman, and she arrested her steps.

"Where do you live, little girl?" she asked, softening her voice as much as practicable, so as not to alarm the child.

"I live there," said the little girl, pointing to the house the woman had just quitted.

"Yes, yes," muttered the latter to herself; "you're the child of that proud lady that refused me what I asked. Perhaps she may repent it."

"Would you like to go with me?" she asked, turning once more to the child. "I will show you where there are flowers a great deal prettier."

"Yes," said the unsuspecting child, gaining her feet, and placing her hand in the woman's.

Was there no magic in the soft touch of that little hand that could turn away that bad woman from her wicked purpose?

Alas! when the heart becomes familiar with crime, all the gentler parts of the nature become hard and callous.

"Would you like to have me take you in my arms, and then we should get there quicker?" said the woman, who knew it would not do to accommodate herself to the child's slow pace.

The latter made no resistance; and, with the little girl in her arms, the woman walked swiftly along. She soon turned aside from the street, for fear of attracting a degree of observation,—which, under present circumstances, would be embarrassing to her,—and took her way, by a less frequented road, to the city.

The child soon became restless, and wished to go home. The woman assured her that she was carrying her there.

Before long, the regular motion of walking acted as a sedative upon the child, and she fell asleep. Her bearer made the most of this opportunity, and walked with quickened steps towards her haunt—for home she had none—in the great city, which she had already entered. Some whom she met gazed with curious eyes at the woman and her burden, and could not help noting the contrast between the two in dress: but no one felt called upon to interfere; and so she reached her destination.

The next day saw Helen—for this the woman discovered to be the child's name—stripped of her tasteful attire, and clothed in a ragged and dirty dress, suited to the company into which she had fallen. At the same time, her abundant curls were cut off close to her head, principally to render more difficult the chance of recognition.

The woman found Helen of essential service in her line. Though disfigured by her uncouth dress and the loss of her curls, her beauty was sufficiently striking to draw many a coin from compassionate strangers, which would not otherwise have been obtained. This little episode completed, we resume the main thread of our narrative.

V.

Notwithstanding the kind treatment which Helen received in her new home, she did not seem happy. Although the companions among which she had been thrown had not been of a nature to give her very elevated ideas of moral rectitude, something within told her that the act required of her would be one of the basest ingratitude. The more she thought of it, the more her heart recoiled from it. Yet so accustomed was she to obey the man Armstrong without question,—not so much from affection as from fear and a sense of duty,—that she had hardly admitted to herself

114

the possibility of refusing to comply with his demands. Now, however, that he had himself confessed that no relationship existed between them, the force of the latter consideration was not a little weakened; and, as fear decreases in the absence of those who inspire it, she began now to consider in what way she could contrive to avoid it.

Circumstances occurred before the dreaded Friday night which served to hasten her decision. On the day previous, while roaming through the fields with Ellen and Frank Gregory, in jumping hastily from a stone wall, her foot turned, and her ankle was severely sprained. The pain was so violent that she nearly fainted, and was quite unable to make her way to the house, which was some quarter of a mile distant. The children were exceedingly frightened, and, returning in breathless haste, gave an immediate alarm.

Two men were speedily obtained, who, constructing a soft litter, conveyed Helen to the house, without occasioning her much additional pain. A physician was at once summoned. Meanwhile, Helen was put to bed, where she received every attention. Mrs. Gregory had a warm heart, which suffering in any form was sure to reach; and, had Helen been her own child, she could not have been more tenderly cared for.

The physician decided that it was nothing very serious; though he recommended, as a necessary precaution, that the injured member should not be used for a fortnight or more, lest inflammation might ensue.

Helen did not hear him pronounce this sentence. When, however, she was informed of it by Mrs. Gregory, after his departure, her mind at once reverted to the fact that it would be an insuperable obstacle to her performing the part assigned her. Actuated by the relief which the thought brought to her, and without thinking of the manner in which it would be construed, she involuntarily exclaimed, —

115

"Oh! I am so glad!"

"Glad!" exclaimed Mrs. Gregory, in astonishment. "What can you mean? You surely cannot mean that you are glad you will be confined to the house by sickness?"

Helen was embarrassed. She knew she could not explain herself without telling all; and that she had not yet determined upon. At length she said, —

"Because it will prevent me from doing something that I did not want to do."

"But why did you not want to do it?" asked Mrs. Gregory.

"Because I do not think it would have been right."

"Then why would you have done it at all, even if you had been well enough, if it was wrong?" asked Mrs. Gregory, more puzzled than ever.

"Because I was afraid to refuse," said Helen, in a low tone.

"It was nothing that I required of you, I am sure," said her mistress.

"No."

"It surely could not be that your grandfather would require of you any thing improper?"

Helen was silent.

"Then it is so. My dear child," pursued the lady, kindly, "I have lived longer than you, and naturally have more knowledge of the world. I need not say that I have every disposition to befriend you, not only for your own sake, but for the sake of my own little Helen, who, had she remained to me, would have been about your age. Will you not, then, confide in me so far as to inform me what it was that your grandfather required of you?"

Helen considered a moment, and then, with a rapidity of decision which sometimes comes after long and anxious thought, decided to communicate every thing.

"I will tell you every thing," she said, "if you will promise that no harm shall come to the man who brought me here."

"Your grandfather?"

"Will you promise?" asked Helen, anxiously.

"Yes, Helen," said Mrs. Gregory: "though I cannot conceive what is to be the nature of your revelation, I will promise that no harm shall befall your grandfather."

"You are so good and kind," said the child, "that I can trust to what you say. Then I will tell you, first of all, that the one who came with me is not my grandfather."

"Not your grandfather?" echoed Mrs. Gregory, in surprise.

"No. He is not even an old man. He only dressed himself up so when he came here."

"And what made him do that?"

"Because he thought you would pity him, and be more ready to take me."

"Is he any relation to you?"

"I thought he was my uncle," returned Helen, "until he came here last time. Then he told me that he was no relation."

"Where are your relations?"

"I don't know," said Helen, thoughtfully. "I suppose I must have had some once; but I can't remember any thing about them. I have lived with my—I mean Mr. Armstrong, ever since I can recollect."

"And what was it he wanted you to do? Why was he so

anxious to have you come here?"

"Because You mustn't blame me," said Helen, earnestly, lifting her eyes to Mrs. Gregory's face; "for it made me very unhappy to think of doing it. But he wanted me to leave the door open to-morrow night, so that he could get in and carry off the silver."

"Is it possible?" exclaimed Mrs. Gregory. "And he wished to implicate you in such a crime?"

"Yes, ma'am," said Helen. "He told me that was what he wanted me to come here for; and then I didn't want to come at all. But he threatened me if I did not. Then, when he was here last time, I tried to persuade him to give up his design; but he wouldn't listen to me, and I didn't dare to say any thing more."

"You said, Helen," remarked Mrs. Gregory, "that you never knew about your relations. Can't you remember any thing that happened when you was a little child?"

"No," said Helen, "not much; but I think I must have lived in the country once, though I can't remember when. There was an old woman, very cross, that I used to be with before Mr. Armstrong took me. She used to beat me sometimes."

"How did she look?" said the lady, feeling a strange interest—for which she found it difficult to account—in the child's story.

"She was very tall; and she used to look at me—oh! so fiercely!"

"And is there nothing, no little keepsake, that you have, to remind you of those childish days?"

"Yes," said Helen, "there was one. It was an ivory ring that I have always carried around with me. The tall woman tried to take it away from me one day; but I cried so that she

118

let me keep it."

"Have you got it with you?" asked Mrs. Gregory, in great agitation.

"Yes," said Helen, surprised at the strange effect this communication appeared to have upon her mistress. "I always carry it in the pocket of my dress."

Mrs. Gregory, with trembling hands, sought the receptacle indicated, and drew out an ivory ring, on which were inscribed the letters "H. G." Without a word, she sprang to the bed, clasped the bewildered Helen to her bosom, and exclaimed, tearfully, —

"It is as I thought! You are my child!—my long-lost Helen!"

When her emotion had in some measure subsided, she made Helen acquainted with the circumstances mentioned in the previous chapter, and also informed her that the ring, which had served as the happy means of restoring a long-lost child to her parent, was the gift of a brother of hers, who had inscribed upon it "H. G.," as the initials of Helen's name, and that the child had it with her on the day of her disappearance.

The happiness of Helen in being restored to her mother, and the joy of the children on ascertaining that the one whom they had learned to love so well, already, was their own sister, may better be imagined than described.

One leaf remains to be added to this chronicle. It relates to Armstrong, hitherto the guardian of Helen. Although the latter had received at his hands so little for which she had occasion to be thankful, she could not reconcile herself to the idea of his being imprisoned. We cannot look with indifference upon the punishment of one with whom we have been intimately associated, however well deserved it may be.

As Armstrong had no intimation of the check which his projects had received, and as he was convinced that Helen's fear of him would lead her to carry out his commands, he stealthily approached the house the following evening, as he had intended. The door had been purposely left unlocked; but, in the room adjoining, four stout men had been stationed, who at once seized upon the unsuspecting burglar, and, in spite of his violent struggles, bound him. Thus secured, Mr. Gregory, who was one of the four, explained to him in what manner his crime had been defeated, and added, —

"Although you have been detected in crime, and richly deserve the penalty which the offended law affixes to it, I have been induced by Helen to afford you a chance of escaping. I will furnish you a ticket entitling you to a passage in the next California steamer, and will not reveal your guilty attempt, if you will engage to leave the country immediately. Should you fail to go, I shall feel released from the promise I have made to Helen, and at once cause you to be arrested."

It is needless to say that Armstrong at once accepted these terms; and the next steamer bound to the Pacific bore him a passenger.

As for Helen, the cloud which shadowed her earlier years has quite disappeared; and in the affection of the home circle, to which her many good qualities endear her, she finds all that can make life pleasant and agreeable.

GERALDINE.

When the summer, crowned with blossoms,
    Robes with beauty all the trees,
And, with pérfumed breath and fragrant,
    Loads the idly-floating breeze,
Then, with cheerful steps and airy,
    O'er the fields with flowers upspringing,
Comes our pleasant household fairy,
    Fragrant blossoms round her flinging,
While the birds that haunt the tree-tops
    Pause to listen to her singing.
Ever cheerful, ever smiling,
    Is the gay, warm-hearted maiden;
And her sunny presence gladdens
    Hearts with deepest sorrow laden.
Very few there are, I ween,
Quite as fair as Geraldine.

When the autumn, — nut-brown autumn, —
    With its wealth of golden sheaves,
Lends a new flush to the apples
    Peeping from the orchard leaves,
Forth unto the sunny harvest
    Rides she in the farmer's wain,
Who, with busy hand and tireless,
    Gathers in the golden grain;
And she cheers his pleasant labor
    With a gay, unstudied strain.
Ever cheerful, ever smiling,
    Is the gay, warm-hearted maiden;
And her sunny presence gladdens
    Hearts with deepest sorrow laden.
Ah! there can be none, I ween,
Quite so fair as Geraldine.

THE CHRISTMAS GIFT.

Heavily, heavily fell the snow, covering the dark-brown earth, already hardened by the frost, with a pure white covering. As the rain falls alike upon the just and upon the unjust; so, too, the snow, God's kindred messenger, knows no distinction of persons,—visiting all alike, forgetting none, and passing by none.

In one of the principal streets of New York stood a boy of some twelve years. His clothing was poor, and too scanty to afford a sufficient protection against the inclemency of the season. Through the visor of his cap, which had become detached in the middle, having a connection only at the two extremities, might be seen his rich brown hair. Notwithstanding the drawback of his coarse and ill-fitting attire, it was evident that he possessed a more than ordinary share of boyish beauty. But just at present his brow is overcast with a shade of anxiety; and his frame trembles with the cold, from which he is so insufficiently shielded.

It is a handsome street, that in which he is standing. On either side he beholds the residences of those on whom Fortune has showered her favors. Bright lights gleam from the parlor windows, and shouts of mirth and laughter ring out upon the night.

All is joy and brightness and festivity within those palace-homes. The snow-flakes fall idly against the window-panes. They cannot chill the hearts within, nor place a bar upon their enjoyment; for this is Christmas Eve, long awaited, at length arrived. Christmas Eve, around which so many youthful anticipations cluster, has enjoyments peculiarly its own, over which the elements, however boisterous, have no control. Yet, to some, Christmas Eve brings more sorrow

125

than enjoyment,—serving only to heighten the contrast between present poverty and discomfort and past affluence.

But all this time we have left our little hero shivering in the street.

Cold and uncomfortable as he was, as well as anxious in mind,—for he had lost his way, and knew not how to find it again,—he could not help forgetting his situation, for the time, in witnessing the scene which met his eye, as, for a moment, he stood in front of a handsome residence on the south side of the street. The curtains were drawn aside; so that, by supporting himself on the railing, he had an unobstructed view of the scene within.

It was a spacious parlor, furnished in a style elegant, but not ostentatious. In the centre of the apartment was a Christmas-tree, brilliant with tapers, which were gleaming from every branch and twig. Gifts of various kinds were hung upon the tree, around which were gathered a group of three children, respectively of eight, six, and four years. The eldest was a winsome fairy, with sparkling eyes and dancing feet. The others were boys, who were making the most of this rare opportunity of sitting up after nine o'clock. At a little distance stood Mr. Dinsmoor and his wife, gazing with unalloyed enjoyment at the happiness of their children.

While Lizzie was indulging in expressions of delight at the superb wax doll which St. Nicholas had so generously provided, her attention was for a moment drawn to the window, through which she distinctly saw the figure of our hero, who, as we have said, had in his eagerness raised himself upon the railing outside, in order to obtain a better view. She uttered an exclamation of surprise.

"Why, mother! there's a boy looking in at the window! Just look at him!"

Mrs. Dinsmoor looked in the direction indicated, and saw the little boy, without his perceiving that attention had been drawn towards him.

"Some poor boy," she remarked to her husband, in a compassionate tone, "who loses for a moment the sensation of his own discomfort in witnessing our happiness. See how eagerly he looks at the tree! which no doubt appears like something marvellous to him."

"Why can't you let him come in?" asked Lizzie, eagerly. "He must be very cold out there, with the snow-flakes falling upon him. Perhaps he would like to have a nearer view of our tree."

"Very well and kindly thought of, my little girl," said Mr. Dinsmoor, placing his hand for a moment upon her clustering locks. "I will follow your suggestion; but I must do it carefully, or he may be frightened, and run away before he knows what are our intentions."

So speaking, Mr. Dinsmoor moved cautiously to the front door, and opened it suddenly. The boy, startled by the sound, turned towards Mr. Dinsmoor with a frightened air, as if fearing that he would be suspected of some improper motive.

"Indeed, sir," said he, earnestly, "I didn't mean any harm; but it looked so bright and cheerful inside that I couldn't help looking in."

"You have done nothing wrong, my boy," said Mr. Dinsmoor, kindly. "But you must be cold here. Come in, and you will have a chance to see more comfortably than you now do."

The boy looked a little doubtful; for to him, neglected as he had been by the rich and prosperous all his life, it was very difficult to imagine that he was actually invited to enter the imposing mansion before him as a guest. Perhaps Mr. Dinsmoor divined his doubts; for he continued, —

"Come: you must not refuse the invitation. There are some little people inside who would be very much disappointed if you should, since it was they who commissioned me to invite you."

"I am sure, sir, I am very much obliged both to them and to you," said the boy, gratefully, advancing towards Mr. Dinsmoor, of whom he had lost whatever little distrust he had at first felt.

A moment afterwards, and the boy stepped within the spacious parlor. To him, whose home offered no attractions, and few comforts, the scene spread before him might well seem a scene of enchantment.

"Lizzie," said Mr. Dinsmoor, "come forward and welcome your guest. I would introduce him to you; but, unluckily, I do not know his name."

"My name is Willie, —Willie Grant," was the boy's reply.

"Then, Willie Grant, this is Miss Lizzie Dinsmoor, who is, I am sure, glad to see you, since it was at her request that I invited you to enter."

Willie raised his eyes timidly, and bent them for a moment on the singularly beautiful child, who had come forward and frankly placed her hand in his.

There is something irresistible in the witchery of beauty; and Willie felt a warm glow crimsoning his cheeks, as for a moment, forgetful of every thing else, he bent his eyes earnestly upon Lizzie. Then another feeling came over him; and, with a look of shame at his scanty and ill-fitting garments, he dropped her hand, and involuntarily shrank back, as if seeking to screen them from sight.

Perceiving the movement, and guessing its cause, Mr.

Dinsmoor, with a view to dissipate these feelings, led forward Harry and Charlie, the younger boys, and told them to make acquaintance with Willie. With loud shouts of delight, they displayed the various gifts which St. Nicholas had brought them, and challenged his admiration.

Every thing was new to Willie. His childhood had not been smiled upon by Fortune; and the costly toys which the boys exhibited elicited quite as much admiration as they could desire.

Occupied in this way, his constraint gradually wore off to such a degree that he assisted Charlie and Harry in trying their new toys. Soon, however, the recollection that it was growing late, and that he had yet to find his way home, came to him; and, taking his old hat, he said to Mr. Dinsmoor, in an embarrassed manner,—

"My mother will be expecting me home; and I should already have been there, but that I lost my way, and happened to look in at your window, and you were so kind as to let me come in."

"Where does your mother live, my little fellow?" asked Mr. Dinsmoor.

"On Street."

"Oh! that is not far off. I will myself show you the way, if you will remain a few minutes longer."

Mr. Dinsmoor rang the bell, and ordered a plate of cake and apples, as he conjectured they would not be unacceptable to his little visitor.

Meanwhile, Lizzie crept to her mother's side, and whispered,—

"Willie is poor,—isn't he?"

"Yes. What makes you ask?"

"I thought he must be, because his clothes look so thin, and patched. Don't you think he would like a Christmas present, mother?"

"Yes, my darling. Have you any thing to give him?"

"I thought, mother, perhaps you would let me give him my five-dollar gold-piece. I think that would be better than any playthings. May I give it?"

"Yes, my child, if you are really willing. But are you quite sure that you would not regret it afterwards?"

"Yes, mother." And Lizzie ran lightly to the little box where she kept her treasure, quickly brought it forth, and placed it in Willie's hand.

"That is your Christmas present," said she, gayly.

Willie looked surprised.

"Do you mean it for me?" he asked, in a half-bewildered tone.

"Yes, if you like it."

"I thank you very much for your kindness," said Willie, earnestly, "and I will always remember it."

There was something in the boy's earnest tone which Lizzie felt was an ample recompense for the little sacrifice she had made. Mr. Dinsmoor fulfilled his promise, and walked with Willie as far as the street in which he lived, when, feeling sure that he could no longer mistake his way, he left him.

Mr. Dinsmoor, whom we have introduced to our readers, was a prosperous merchant, and counted his wealth by hundreds of thousands. Fortunately, his disposition was liberal; and he made the poor sharers with him in the gifts which Fortune had so liberally showered upon him.

Notwithstanding the good use which he made of his wealth, he was fated to experience reverses,—resulting, not from his own mismanagement, but from a general commercial panic, which all at once involved in ruin many whose fortunes were large, and whose credit was long established. In a word, Mr. Dinsmoor failed.

———

Eleven years had rolled by since the Christmas night on which our story opens. Lizzie had not belied the promise of her girlhood, but had developed into a radiantly beautiful girl. Already her hand had been sought in marriage; but, as yet, she had seen no one on whom she could look with that affection without which marriage would be a mockery.

Charlie and Harry, too,—eleven years had changed them not a little. The boys of four and six had become fine, manly youths of fifteen and seventeen. The eldest had entered college. Harry, however, who was by no means studious, had entered his father's counting-room.

That was a sorrowful night on which Mr. Dinsmoor made known to his afflicted wife the bankruptcy which was inevitable. Still sadder, if possible, was the sale which it enforced of the house which they had so long occupied, the furniture which had become endeared to them by memory and association, and the harsh interruption which loss of fortune put to all their treasured schemes.

"My poor boy," said Mrs. Dinsmoor, sorrowfully, as she placed her hand caressingly on the brown locks of Charlie, the eldest of the two boys, "it will be a hard sacrifice for you to leave the studies to which you are so much attached, and enter a store, as you will be obliged to do."

"Ah! I had not thought of that," murmured Charlie. "It

131

will, indeed, be a sacrifice; but, mother, I would not care for that, if you could only be spared the trials to which you will be exposed from poverty."

"Thank you for your consideration, my child; but do not fear that I shall not accommodate myself to it. It is a heavy trial; but we must try to think that it will ultimately eventuate in our good."

At the auction of Mr. Dinsmoor's house and furniture, the whole property, without exception, was knocked off to a young man, who seemed apparently of twenty-two or three years of age. He was able to secure it at a price much beneath its real value; for times were hard, and money scarce, so that he had but few competitors. Mr. Dinsmoor did not hear his name, and the pressure of sad thoughts prevented his making the inquiry.

Possession was to be given in one week. Meanwhile, Mr. Dinsmoor sought out a small house in an obscure part of the town, which, in point of elegance and convenience, formed a complete contrast to the one he had formerly occupied. He felt, however, that it would be all his scanty salary as clerk—for he had secured a situation in that capacity—would enable him to afford.

Lizzie looked, with a rueful face, at the piano, as a dear friend from whom she must henceforth be separated, it being quite too costly a piece of furniture to be retained in their reduced circumstances. Her proficiency in music, for which she had great taste, made her regret it doubly, since she might with it have added to the resources of the family by giving music lessons.

On the last evening in which they were to remain in the old house, their sad thoughts were broken in upon by a ring at the bell.

"Can they not even leave us to enjoy the last evening in

quiet?" said Charles, half petulantly.

Immediately afterwards, there entered a young man, in whom Mr. Dinsmoor recognized the purchaser of the house.

"I need not bid you welcome," said he, smiling faintly, "since you have a better right here now than myself. Had I been told, three months since, that this would be, I would not have believed it; but we cannot always foresee. I shall be prepared to leave to-morrow."

"I shall be better satisfied if you will remain," said the young man, bowing.

"What do you mean?"

"Simply, that as this house and furniture are now mine, to do with as I like, I choose to restore you the latter, and offer you the use of the former, rent free, as long as you choose to occupy it."

"Who, then, are you," asked Mr. Dinsmoor, in increasing surprise, "who can be so kind to utter strangers, with no claim upon you?"

"You are mistaken. You have a claim upon me. Shall I tell you what it is? Eleven years ago to-morrow,—for to-morrow is Christmas Day,—a poor boy, who had known none of the luxuries, and but few of the comforts, of life, stood in this street. His mind was ill at ease; for he had lost his way: but, as he walked on, he beheld a blaze of light issuing from a window,—from *your* window,—and, aroused by curiosity, he looked in. Around a Christmas-tree, brilliant with light, a happy group were assembled. As he stood gazing in, he heard the front door open; and a gentleman came out, and kindly invited him to enter. He did so; and the words of kindness and the Christmas gift with which he departed have not yet left his remembrance. Seven years passed, and the boy's fortune changed. An uncle, long

133

supposed to be dead, found him out, and, when he actually died, left him the heir of a large amount of wealth. Need I say that I am that boy, and that my name is Willie Grant?"

The reader's imagination can easily supply the rest. Provided with capital by his young friend, Mr. Dinsmoor again embarked in business; and, this time, nothing occurred to check his prosperity. Charlie did *not* leave college, nor did Lizzie lose her piano. She gained a husband, however, and had no reason to regret the train of events which issued from her CHRISTMAS GIFT.

MY PICTURE.

I have a beautiful picture;
   And gorgeous are its dyes,
Wherein the green of the meadows
   Blends with the blue of the skies.

A forest stands in the background;
   And hills are at the sides;
And a valley lies between them,
   Through which a streamlet glides.

There are fields that teem with a harvest
   Of rich and ripening grain,
That has caught the glow of the sunlight,
   And will not return it again;—

There are broad and spacious pastures,
   Where the quiet cattle stray,
And the schoolboys meet to play at ball
   On their weekly holiday;—

While here and there a cottage
   Peeps out from the leafy lane;
And through the trees you can catch a glimpse
   Of the farmer with his wain.

And out in the dark old forest
   There is many a stately tree,
That has seen the green leaves come and go
   For more than a century.

I have heard of the ancient masters,
   I have heard of their marvellous skill,
And how the dull, dead canvas
   Would glow with life at their will;—

But, when the sunshine falleth
   The rifts of the cloudlets through,
It lends to my picture a glory
   That Raphael never knew.

And, when the solemn moonlight
   Looks down with its mellow shine,
My picture is bathed in beauty
   That seemeth almost divine.

And whenever I gaze at my picture,
   Whether sun or stars light the sky,
I feel that my spirit is strengthened,
   And my heart is made richer thereby.

GOTTFRIED THE SCHOLAR.

Alone in his study sat Gottfried the scholar. The shelves which lined the apartment on every side groaned beneath the weight of bulky quartoes and ponderous folios. The accumulated learning of many ages and countries, flowing in diverse channels, had mingled into one stream, and, with its fertilizing current, contributed to enrich the mind of Gottfried. And these many volumes, couched in languages which to all but their owner were a sealed book, which many years' assiduous labor and midnight vigils alone could unclose,—these were but the index of Gottfried's attainments.

Never in the palmiest days of chivalry had knight been more constant to his mistress than Gottfried to his books. Without these, life would have been to him a blank, and the world a desert. What to him were the companionship of friends, the charms of social intercourse? He recognized no friends but his books; and with them alone he held intercourse. He had cultivated his intellect to the neglect of his heart: beneath his fostering care, the former had swelled into the proportions of a giant; the latter, like an untilled garden, had been abandoned to the rank growth of weeds, which had already overshadowed it, and checked the growth of kind feelings and human affections.

But of this defect Gottfried was not conscious; or, at least, he would not have acknowledged it to be such. With all his wisdom, he knew not the meaning of virtue; for he was perpetually confounding it with learning; so that with him the philosophy of life might be said to consist in these few words: "To be learned is to be virtuous." Thus it was, that, in the pride of his attainments, he looked down upon other

137

men as immeasurably his inferiors, and was even half convinced that they were of a different nature from himself.

He aspired to become in the world of intellect what Alexander was in the physical world, and, like that monarch, sighed to think that there were no more worlds to conquer,—no more victories to be gained.

Gottfried had just written the concluding paragraph of a treatise upon some abstruse subject, which possessed an interest only for scholars like himself. His pen dropped wearily from his fingers, and he passed his hand across his eyes.

"Yes," said he, musingly, and a smile lighted up his face, "at length it is finished, the labor of many years. But the reward is to come. My fame as a scholar, already great among men, will become greater still. Fame, bright goddess of my youthful dreams! how through weary years have I toiled for thee! How willingly have I resigned those objects on which other men set their affections! Wealth, pleasure, love,—I have sacrificed them all to this one engrossing pursuit. Who shall say that I have lived in vain?"

Gottfried had labored for many hours without rest. He took down his scholar's cap and cloak from the wall against which they were suspended, and attired himself for a walk.

It was a beautiful day. The sun had passed the meridian, and was shining with softened splendor on fields decorated with the green carpet which Nature so bounteously provides. Here a group of cattle reposed in tranquil enjoyment beneath the spreading branches of trees, which afforded a grateful shelter from the sun's heat. A little farther on, a tiny stream was seen rippling on its way. Beside it were childish figures playfully plucking the flowers that grew upon the banks, and tossing them into the water, where they were soon borne down the quick current. Children, however small, have an eye to the beautiful; and the little group sang and shouted in all the exuberance of their spirits. The smile of outward nature was reflected upon the faces of these little ones.

As Gottfried passed by, one of them, supposing that all must share in her feelings, plucked a flower, and, holding it up, exclaimed, "Is it not pretty?"

"What is pretty?" asked Gottfried, looking up.

The flower was held up in answer. "Poh! child: it is only a buttercup."

The child drew back abashed, and Gottfried pursued his way. He regarded not the fair landscape which like a dream of beauty opened upon his steps. His mind was still at home among his books. Indeed, it rarely passed beyond those four dark walls wherein all that he cared for in life was enclosed. With the laws of Nature, so far as they had been ascertained by human wisdom, he was thoroughly conversant; but for Nature itself he cared little. He could tell you all that science has discovered of the mysterious courses of the heavenly bodies; but the finest evening that ever looked down with its thousand glittering eyes from the blue vault above vainly tempted him forth from his study. He would have regarded it as a mere weakness to yield to such an impulse. He at least was in no danger of yielding; for he never felt the impulse.

Gottfried passed on, plunged as before in deep thought, of which the treatise which he had just completed was the absorbing subject.

A woman with a babe in her arms, whose melancholy face and tattered garb spoke sadly of unhappiness and destitution, stood in the path. He would not have noticed her, had she not timidly touched the hem of his garment.

"Why do you disturb me?" he asked impatiently, as he

139

looked up. "You have interrupted the current of my thoughts. What would you have?"

"I hope, sir," said the woman, in a low tone, "you will pardon the interruption. I would not willingly intrude; but you see my situation. I am left destitute, and without friends. For myself, I care not. Perhaps it is well that I should die; but my child,—I would live for him."

Gottfried listened with an unmoved countenance, and as one who but half comprehended what he heard.

"If you are poor and in distress," he said at length, "you can apply to the proper authorities. I have matters of more importance to attend to."

"Of more importance than the life of a fellow-creature?" interrupted a rough-looking man, in a farmer's dress, who had just stepped up. "Nay, then, I have not. Come with me, my poor woman. I live in the cottage yonder. It is but a poor place; but it will afford you food and shelter."

"Such men," mused Gottfried, "do not estimate the superiority of science over the trivial objects upon which most waste their lives to little purpose. But how should they? They pass their lives in a round of petty duties and petty employments, above and beyond which they care not to look."

Such were the meditations of Gottfried. Ah! thou that canst see the mote in thy brother's eye, and dost not discern the beam that is in thine own!

Gottfried was approaching his study on his return from the walk, when his meditations were disturbed by a cry which always makes the blood course more quickly through the veins,—the fearful cry of "Fire!" Voice after voice took up the cry till it swelled into a terrible and confused clamor. Fire! Gottfried looked up, and, to his inexpressible

140

consternation, beheld the flames rapidly consuming his own dwelling. The conviction flashed upon him, with the speed of lightning, that he had left a candle burning which he had lighted for the purpose of sealing a letter. Undoubtedly it had come in contact with the loose papers which lay about it, and *this* was the result.

"My books! my treatise!" exclaimed Gottfried with anguish, as he contemplated the probability of their destruction. "They will all be consumed!"

He hurried to the scene of disaster. The firemen were plying their utmost efforts to bring the flames under. But the fire had already made such headway that they struggled against hope.

Gottfried lent his aid with the energy of despair. Finally, unable to conceal from himself that the building must be consumed, he rushed into the crackling flames, in the hope of at least rescuing the manuscript of which he had written that day the concluding paragraphs.

It was a mad effort, such as nothing but despair could prompt. The smoke stifled him; the flames scorched and burned him. He was dragged out by main force, having succeeded in passing but a few feet beyond the threshold. Luckily he was in a state of insensibility, so that the last scenes in the conflagration passed without his knowledge.

The weeks that succeeded were a blank to Gottfried, for he was plunged in the delirium of a brain fever. When, at length, he awoke to consciousness, it was in a small and poorly-furnished chamber. At the bedside was seated a woman, coarsely but neatly attired.

"Where am I?" he inquired, bewildered. "What has happened to me?"

"You are at length better, thank Heaven," said the

woman, earnestly, "since the delirium has left you."

"Delirium!" said Gottfried, raising himself on his elbow in surprise. "Oh, yes! I now recall the fearful calamity which has befallen me. My books,—are they all gone? Is there not one left?"

"Yes, one was saved."

"What is it? Bring it to me."

From a shelf near by, the attendant took down a small volume which had been scorched, but not otherwise injured, by the flames.

He opened it. It proved to be the New Testament in the original tongue. Perhaps out of his whole library this was the book which he had least studied. Now, however, that it was all that was left him, he passed hours in its perusal. Gradually, as he read, a light broke in upon him; and he began to perceive, at first by glimpses, but after a while with all the clearness of light, that his life had been a mistake, and that learning was not, as he had fancied, the great end of existence. He perceived that in its attainment he had neglected what were of infinitely more importance,—his duties to God and his fellow-men. With a feeling of humiliation, he could not but confess that his life had been in vain.

One day, as he was rapidly approaching recovery, he turned to his nurse, and said, abruptly,—

"Where have I met you before? Your face looks familiar."

"On the day of the fire," was the reply, "you met me and my little one. We were destitute, and implored charity."

"Which I denied. Yet you nurse me with all the devotedness of one who is serving a benefactor. How is this?"

"I am only doing my duty. But it is not to me you are indebted: it is to the good farmer whose hospitality we both alike share."

"Is it possible?" said Gottfried, with humiliation. "It is, then, he over whom I triumphed in fancied superiority. With all the learning which I have gathered from books, I feel, that, in the true wisdom of life, I am vastly inferior to you both."

On his recovery, Gottfried again applied himself to his studies; but henceforth he never sought to elevate mere worldly knowledge above "that wisdom which passeth all understanding."

INNOCENCE.

Contributed by a friend.

The blue sky was her canopy;
   The flower-gemmed turf, her shrine;
Her incense, deep and fervent love,
   Pure from the heart's rich mine.

Her brow was fair, her eyes were mild,
   Her sunny smile was bright:
No discontent its shadow threw
   Across her spirit's light.

Angels their constant vigil kept,
   And guarded her from harm;
Breathing around her, while she slept,
   A spirit-soothing charm.

But she hath left this guilt-stained earth:
   No more her smiles may cheer;
No more her gentle voice of mirth
   May breathe its music here.

Her haunts are desecrated now,
   Or desolate and lone;
And Psyche's palace, where she dwelt,
   Has ceased to be her home.

PETER PLUNKETT'S ADVENTURE.

Some years since, there lived in Portland a worthy shoemaker named Peter Plunkett. Unpoetical as his name may appear, Peter possessed a vivid imagination, which, had it been properly cultivated, might have made him, perchance, a poet or a novelist. As it was, he chiefly employed it in building air-castles of more than royal magnificence, wherein dwelt fairies and genii. If there was any book that approached the Bible, in Peter's estimation, it was the "Arabian Nights' Entertainments." He had a devout belief in all the marvellous stories which it contains, and often sighed in secret that it had not been his fortune to live in the days of that potent monarch,—the Caliph Haroun Al Raschid.

Peter Plunkett's peculiarity was well known. Indeed, his mind was most of the time far back in the golden age of fairies, so that he would sometimes be guilty of amusing mistakes. On one occasion, he addressed his housekeeper as "Most charming princess!" whereupon the good woman was led to entertain serious doubts as to his sanity, which, indeed, were not wholly unreasonable, since, though an excellent cook, she certainly did not look much like a princess.

Not far from Peter's shop lived Squire Eveleth, who, being mirthfully inclined, resolved to take advantage of the worthy shoemaker's fancies, and play upon him a practical joke.

Happening into Peter's shop, he led the conversation to the subject of genii. "I have sometimes thought," said he, gravely, "that the fairies and genii have not yet abandoned the earth, but still continue, invisibly to us, to exercise an

145

influence over our destinies."

"So have I," said Peter, eagerly. "Many a time I have fancied, as I sat here at work, that I could hear the rushing of their wings as they circled about me; and I have sometimes invoked them to appear in visible form; but they never have."

"Perhaps they will some time," said the squire, encouragingly. "I wish you would come and take tea with me to-morrow," he continued, after a pause. "I should like to confer with you about these things."

Consent was readily accorded; and the next afternoon found Peter Plunkett a guest of the squire. The latter, unperceived, mingled a potion with Peter's tea; and the result was that in half an hour he was in a sound sleep. In this condition, the squire had him conveyed in a carriage to the depot; and, in a few minutes, they were travelling towards Boston. They reached the city in the evening; and Peter, still sleeping, was conveyed to the Revere House, carried to a bed-chamber, and deposited in bed. Squire Eveleth then retired, and, after leaving a note on the table, left the house; and, after passing the night at another hotel, returned, in the morning train, to Portland.

The sun was already high in the heavens when Peter Plunkett awoke. He gazed, bewildered, at the unwonted appearance of the room, and, jumping out of bed, walked mechanically to the window.

"Surely this can't be Portland," he said to himself, as the towers and steeples of Boston met his view. "Where am I? What can have happened to me?"

Turning from the window, his eye rested upon a letter lying upon the table, addressed to himself.

He opened it hastily, and read as follows: —

146

"MORTAL! be thankful; for to you, in return for your unquestioning faith, has been vouchsafed a favor which distinguishes you above your fellow-men. I who write to you am Aldabaran, the potent genie of the air. Last night, I snatched you from your couch, in the dead of night, and bore you hither. You are now at the Revere House, in Boston. In your pocket you will find gold, which I have placed there. It will defray all your expenses, and bear you back to Portland. But beware lest you divulge to any one the chance that has befallen you; for, should you be so indiscreet, I swear to you by Solomon's seal, which glows with unapproachable splendor, that you will instantly be transformed into a gigantic jackass, and be doomed in that shape to walk the earth for ever as the penalty of your folly.

"Farewell, and beware!

"ALDABARAN."

As Peter Plunkett read this terrible missive, his hair stood on end with affright; yet, in the midst of his terror, he was filled with joy at the nature of the favor which had been granted him.

That night, he returned to Portland. Many curious inquiries were made of him as to the object of his journey; for this was the first time he had left Portland for many years. To all these inquiries he preserved an impenetrable silence; merely shaking his head mysteriously, lest he should incur the dreadful doom denounced against him. Henceforth he deemed himself as one singled out from the great mass of mankind. Upon his fellow-mortals he looked with a pitying eye, as beings with whom the invisible spirits of the air had never deigned to hold communication. Happy in his innocent delusion, he would not exchange places with the most powerful monarch. Locked up in his trunk are the gold coins which he found in his pocket in accordance with the mysterious letter. He will never spend them; for he regards them as a fairy gift; and he fancies, that, while he holds them in his possession, Fortune will ever smile upon him.

THE END.